I0748000

THE WOLF'S SONG

Bite of Magic – Book 3

LUCILLE YATES

Book and Cover design by Maria Spada
Edits by Red Light Remy
Book Formatting Template by Derek Murphy @Creativindie
Least of My Kind © 1994 by Catherine Faber used with permission

First Edition: October 2022

ISBN: 9781736969793

Kitty Hex Press

www.lucilleyateswrites.com

DEDICATION

To my sister.
To my first beta reader, my best friend, and one of the
few people who will tell me the absolute truth. Thank
you so much for your support.

CHAPTER 1

Spencer

Spencer looked around the building in the dusk of the setting sun. Mondays in Savannah tended to be busy, but at the moment, he couldn't see anyone around. Spencer called his wolf to the forefront of his mind. He knew his eyes had changed and felt the hair on his face lengthen. He sniffed the air. Nothing but trees, exhaust, and dog piss filled his nose. He moved to the other corner of the building and scented the same thing. Whoever entered the shop covered their scent. With a deep sigh, he continued across the back and into the next yard, sniffing every few feet. As he approached the street on the other side of the building, he pulled back his wolf. He stepped onto the sidewalk, sniffing the air. His sense of smell couldn't match that of his wolf, but far surpassed that of a regular human. Nothing still.

Shaking his head, he turned to take the long way back to Herbs and Healing. He turned the corner when his phone rang.

He looked at the caller. Keon. Shit. He forgot to meet him downtown for open mic night and failed to call him when the emergency arrived.

"Hey Keon." He cringed at his own nonchalant tone.

"Where are you? Or did you forget?" Keon's voice sounded short.

"I forgot to call you." Spencer sighed. "Someone attacked Maggie at her shop. I'm helping track him down."

"Oh shit! Do y'all need help? I can be there in five minutes."

"No. I think there are enough people here. But there is no way I can meet you. They are going to go over a protection plan soon."

"And they're going to rope you into it."

"Unfortunately, but I don't mind. Maggie's like family."

"Didn't someone break into her shop last week, too?" The background noise on Keon's end became louder.

"Yeah. But they didn't take anything or break anything. Maggie is convinced it was just a crime of convenience."

"I bet she doesn't feel that way now."

"Nope. And the weird part is, they don't have a smell. I can't track them."

"Or you're off your game."

"Excuse me? You've lost your damn mind. I'm top of my game. I'm top of your game."

"Is that why you forgot to call?" He could hear Keon

smiling.

"Alright. I gotta go. Go find us a lead singer. I'll call you later."

Spencer shook his head as he walked back to the shop. The lead singer for their band moved a week ago, and they couldn't find a replacement they liked. The band wasn't fantastic, but they had standards. After putting ads up around town and auditioning six people, they resorted to going to open mic nights, hoping to run into someone acceptable.

He'd have to rely on Keon's taste to find someone. This was the third open mic he'd missed. Between his jobs, the pack, and the band, his schedule was full. If only they could get rid of the Cernunnos hunters, life would slow down, and he'd be able to breathe again.

He hopped up on the porch of the brick building south of Forsyth Park and walked into the shop. The store front looked so different since Maggie's cousin, Jesi, opened her law firm on the top floor, adding a second door to the front. After the third time of him 'pretending' to walk through the wrong door, Jesi threatened to shave his head in his sleep. He could use the haircut, but he didn't want a bald head. He also wouldn't put it past his sister to let Jesi into his house.

Speaking of his sister, Emma, she stood with her arms around everyone's favorite almost-witch, Maggie. Her now blue hair fell just below her ears, her lips pulled tight, and her eyes looked puffy. He'd never seen her with tear-stained cheeks.

The brightly decorated shop looked wrong at that

moment, or were the solemn looks on everyone's faces out of place? Everything felt wrong. The pack leader, Ethan, stood next to the coven leader, Sylvia. He couldn't hear anything they said to each other. Keon's dad, Isaiah, talked to Maggie and Emma. He knew others from his pack were still canvassing the neighborhood. He heard a few voices floating in from the 'Real Magic' room, which Maggie disguised as a storage room for anyone unconnected to the supernatural.

He walked over to Isaiah, content to wait for Ethan to finish his conversation with Ms. Sylvia.

Isaiah and Emma both raised their eyebrows at him. He shook his head.

"He must be using something to mask his scent," he frowned. "But it smells wonderful in here. Are you burning a new candle?"

He'd never expected to enjoy a sweet sandalwood scent, but he wanted whatever product the smell came from. He tried to pinpoint it, but it didn't seem to come from any one direction.

Maggie sucked in a deep breath and shook off Emma. "I'm okay now," she said. "I'm usually so prepared. I was prepared. He must have had anti magic shields or something."

"How did you fight him off?"

"I kicked him in the dick, then elbowed him in the face. After that I pulled my iron knife and he ran off."

"That's my girl." Emma squeezed her again.

The door which led to Maggie's workshop opened and out walked Jesi, her cousin, and her boyfriend, Chuck.

Chuck worked as a detective for the local police department. He kissed Jesi on the cheek.

"I'll take the footage over to the precinct. Maybe we can get a good shot of his face and run the facial recognition software." He waved and left.

Jesi pulled up a seat and sat on the other side of the counter, her head resting in her hand.

"They'll try a different tactic next time," Ethan said, joining the group with Sylvia.

"What do they want with me? Are they still after that book?" Maggie shook her head and pushed air through her nose in a huff.

"Their desires are immaterial. Your safety must take precedence. You will no longer travel unaccompanied." Sylvia stared at her niece, Maggie.

Spencer raised an eyebrow at Ethan who rolled his eyes. Sylvia's way of speaking annoyed most of the wolves.

"Sylvia is right. We need to keep Maggie safe. We will make a list of people willing to help out and create a schedule tomorrow morning. Emma, can you stay with her tonight?"

"You can't be serious?" Maggie's wide eyes glanced between Ethan and Sylvia. "I don't need a babysitter."

"Normally, I'd agree with you, but we don't want to take any chances. This hunter group is getting bolder. We can't take any more chances with either of our people."

"You are more pivotal than you believe. Your safety must be guaranteed." Sylvia squeezed Maggie's hand.

Spencer frowned at the group. He knew Maggie was

strong and knowledgeable, but he didn't know why Sylvia suddenly treated her as critical. Maggie wasn't even a natural witch. She could do magic, but it wasn't innate. She had to follow the old spells, go through the rituals, use the herbs, and say the words to do anything of note. How was she more important than any of the other members of the coven?

Maggie rolled her eyes. "You're not going to scare me into complying. I can take care of myself."

"And you'll do an even better job with backup." Ethan put a hand on her shoulder. "It won't last long. It's for your safety and your aunt's peace of mind."

Maggie's shoulders sank. "No. I refuse. I have a life that I won't let the rest of you interfere in, at least with what you don't already meddle with. I will take extra precautions and people are welcome to come by and check on me, but I don't need a secret service team. The last thing I need is to meet someone and have y'all ruin it for me."

"What makes you think we'd ruin it for you?" Spencer grinned. "We'll be there to take pictures to show your children."

"Spencer's not allowed to be on the list. Not if he wants to keep his balls." She crossed her arms with a glare at him.

Emma laughed, patting Spencer on the shoulder. "My brother doesn't need his balls anyway."

"But my ball collection is what I hold most dear. Can I at least keep my baseball signed by Hank Aaron?"

"Wait, you have MY Hank Aaron baseball?" Emma

turned on him.

"All the balls are MINE!"

"Children," Ethan warned. "Stop playing. Emma, stay with Maggie tonight. Spencer, you can walk the area again. Cover at least five blocks out. The rest of you help the coven with whatever else they need."

Chapter 2

Clare

The light almost blinded Clare from where she stood. The minuscule crowd no longer existed. Her hand wrapped around the neck of her guitar, the other hand poised to strum, and a calm washed over her.

With a deep breath, she strummed the instrument. She set the fast tempo out of the gate and leaned into the mic. Her voice hushed the room. The chorus hit, and the audience came alive, singing along and dancing. "Sugar, We're Going Down" never disappointed on open mic night back home. Clare grinned into the mic, realizing she landed the same reaction here in Savannah.

Sweat trickled down her face as she played in the spotlight. With only ten minutes to play, she quickly transitioned into her next song, hoping to squeeze in a third before they kicked her off for the next act.

She missed having a full band behind her. College life gave her the opportunity to play with others. The beat of the drums filled her chest back then. But jobs spread the band apart and now she found contentment in open mic night.

Her set ended, and she unplugged her guitar, grabbed her pedal, and stepped off the stage, careful not to trip on the cords. The dim club didn't look as empty as when she started. Greeted by smiling faces and handshakes, she knew she'd found a place to play. Once a month would settle her soul. Turned out Monday night mic night drew a decent crowd. She put away River, her guitar, and found a seat.

She listened to the crooning of the country singer on stage. It wasn't her favorite style, but his voice wasn't bad. Clare closed her eyes and nodded along to the song.

"May I sit down?"

The voice brought her away from her musings. A man sat across the small table from her without waiting for her answer. He leaned forward and placed his drink down. He looked up at the stage.

"You have a great stage presence." He sipped his drink.

"Thanks." She looked around the room. No one looked at them. "Who are you?"

He turned and smiled. White teeth flashed against his dark skin. "I'm Keon. And I like the way you sing. I like the music you play and I think you'd be a great fit."

She leaned back, wrapping her hand around the handle of her case. "Fit for what?"

"My band." His eyes laughed. "Our lead moved for a job and we've been looking for a replacement. I'd like you to audition."

"Me?" She scrunched her eyes and frowned. "I'm going to need more details."

"I'm on drums. We have a bass and a lead guitar that sings backup. None of us are good enough to sing lead. And if you don't mind stepping back to rhythm guitar while singing, I think it might work. Of course, the others would have to agree."

"How often do you practice? How often do you perform? Is there any compensation? And how come you're the only one scoping out talent?" She lifted her chin with a smirk.

"Sounds like you've done this before." He gulped down his drink. "We practice twice during the work week with a long practice on Saturdays. The week before a performance, we practice more. We like to perform at least once a month if we can manage. We do clubs and the occasional private party. It's mostly for fun. Occasionally we'll get paid, but it's not much, so don't quit your day job." He chuckled and watched the country singer close his act.

Clare took a good look at him. He leaned back in the chair, watching the stage change musicians. A slight smile never left his face. She never felt the need to leave while he sat across from her. She took her hand off the case and leaned on the table.

"How many other people have you asked to audition?"

"Six before tonight that weren't good fits. I have two more set up. You'd be number nine." He glanced at her. "You interested?"

"I might be."

He reached in his pocket and pulled out a card, placing it on the table. "My number's on the back, if you're interested, but you'll need to let me know within the next few days."

"How do I know I can trust you?"

"Everyone trusts me. I have a trusting face. I give off an aura of friendship."

She laughed. "Someone's been lying to you."

He stood up with a laugh. "I knew I'd like you."

"What's the name of your band?"

"Wolves on Fire." He turned and walked through the growing crowd.

She grabbed the card. The front said Massey and Sons Automotive, but he wrote his name and number on the back in neat penmanship. A smile crept up on her face. She wanted to be on stage with a band behind her once again. She pulled out her phone and searched the name of the band.

Social media links and a website popped up. All legit, with Keon's face mixed in the photos. She'd call him in two days. Maybe she'd call tomorrow. She just hoped all the members were as nice as they were hot, especially the lead guitar. He looked deliciously dangerous, especially in the videos where he played. She could see the lean muscles in his arms and the focus on his face. He was the best kind of eye candy and the worst thing for her heart. Clare laughed at herself. She wasn't looking, not now. It's not like he'd fall instantly in love with her.

Chapter 3

Roderic

Two men sat across from Roderic. He leaned back in his new leather chair, legs crossed, and studied them. His right-hand man, Andre, hung his bald head back and looked at the ceiling. He wasn't big on meetings. The other man, Gunther, sat straight as a board, wearing the official Cernunnos polo shirt. His hands tightly gripped the arms of the chair.

"Andre, what's your status?" Roderic tapped his chin as he spoke.

Andre looked away from the ceiling. "The bounty is in place. And the drop off location is being monitored."

"And Gunther, your status?" Roderic tilted his head toward the second man.

"We have a location on the target. The latent tracking spell is in place. I will personally let you know if it stops working." He barely moved while he spoke.

"Perfect. Keep monitoring her. You may leave."

"Thank you, Mr. Kahn." Gunther stood and nodded

his head.

Roderic watched him leave. When the door shut, he let out a laugh. "Why do you think they like buzz cuts so much?"

Andre smirked. "I told them it was expected of their rank."

"Amusing. That's why I like you. Now, let's discuss information extraction techniques."

~

Spencer

"You are the worst at picking musicians. I think it's because you're a drummer. All rhythm and no melody." Spencer plopped down on the couch in Keon's apartment.

"Then you go scouting for talent." Keon threw a pillow at Spencer.

"You said there's one more person to hear?" Tick shook their head.

"Yes, thank you, Tick, for bringing that up. She should be here in about ten minutes."

"She?" Spencer grinned at Keon. "I thought we agreed we wanted this to be a male vocal band?"

"We did agree to that," Tick said. "Though it was mostly because Dan was so insistent at the time."

"I know, but I want you to hear her. She had a powerful voice and a great stage presence. We don't have to stick to what we decided in high school. We owe it to ourselves to replace Dan with the best possible person."

"Dan is going to flip out when he finds out you want to replace him with a woman." Spencer shook his head and laughed.

The four of them formed this band during their junior year in high school. Four werewolves put their love of music together eight years ago. At sixteen years old, they wanted to have male vocals. Even Tick agreed, stating they couldn't sing, so they were happy to stick with a male lead.

But things changed over eight years. Dan took a job in Huntsville. If they wanted to keep the band alive, they needed a vocalist. Keon wanted Spencer to move into that spot, but he didn't have enough faith in his own voice. Singing backup and playing lead guitar suited him just fine. Plus, of all the members of the group, Spencer spent most time away delivering special materials to other packs. Dan could always cover for Spencer when his two jobs conflicted.

Spencer groaned and stood up. He didn't have much faith in this next musician, anyway. Keon liked anyone who could play and carry a tune, but they rarely met his and Tick's standards.

He walked out of the living room and straight into the kitchen. The others walked out into the garage. They always played at Keon's. He lived centrally located to the rest of them, not in the sticks, like Spencer. Even when Keon bought his own house, their practice location moved with him. Few of Keon's neighbors complained if they practiced early enough.

Spencer took down a glass from the cabinet and filled it with water. He shook his head and considered how many open mic nights he'd need to attend to find a suitable replacement. He'd already talked to the others about running an ad on social media, but they wanted to stake out the various bars for talent first.

After he downed the water, he walked into the garage. The warm breeze blew through the open garage door. It felt wonderful after such a hot day. Looking out the door, he watched a woman holding a guitar case turn at the end of the driveway and head toward them. She must be their last audition of the evening.

Her walk up the driveway stole his attention. The slow setting sun highlighted her shoulder-length black hair and dark amber skin. She wore jeans with holes in the knees, a red tank top, short boots, and a tattoo adorned her upper right arm. When she looked up, she smiled, but not at him. Her brown eyes lit up at the sight of Keon. An unfamiliar fire grew in Spencer's chest, with a wish that she'd look at him with the same delight.

A breeze blew her hair around her face, bringing her scent straight to him. His wolf stirred inside and watched her now. The smell of sandalwood and buttercream awoke something inside of him. The burning in his chest made sense now.

Mate.

This beautiful musician which Keon found was his other half, and he hers. He breathed her in more. Human. Not great for the band, but they could get permission from the pack leader to tell her. He shook his head. She was his mate. He didn't need permission to tell her.

"Hey, Clare," Keon shook her hand.

"Hi." She smiled and looked around at the rest of the group. Her smile faltered a bit when she looked at him.

Tick elbowed him in the ribs. His mouth snapped shut, and he wiped what could only be drool off his lips.

"Clare, this is Tick, who plays bass, and Spencer, who plays lead guitar."

"It's nice to meet everyone."

"If you want to get warmed up, you can put your stuff over here." Keon led her to a bit of floor space where she could get her guitar out.

"Are you okay?" Tick whispered to Spencer.

"What? Yeah." He nodded and looked down at them and their blue pixie hair.

"Your hand is shaking, you're staring, and you haven't made a crack about her. Your job is to tease the newbies. Where is your wit, man? You're supposed to make me laugh."

"I'm not here for your amusement."

"Actually, that's exactly why you're here." They grinned at him, then walked to the back of the garage.

Clare stood to the side, tuning the gorgeous guitar in her hands by ear. Her long fingers gripped the neck as he watched. He could tell by how she moved her fingers that she had years of experience playing. His wolf sent images of those same hands running through his fur. Spencer wanted those hands around his cock.

"Stop staring at her," Keon hissed. "You're gonna freak her out."

He looked away. "Sorry."

Keon pulled him to the back of the garage just before Clare began.

Keon nodded at her, and she nodded back. She whispered, 'one, two, three, four,' under her breath and began to play. Her strumming flowed out of the amp and engulfed the three of them. When her voice joined in, Spencer's and Tick's mouths dropped. The power behind her sound, accompanied by her impeccable guitar skill, blew them away. Keon grinned over at his bandmates, showing all his teeth.

That son of a bitch tricked us, thought Spencer. Honestly, he didn't need to have two ill qualified people audition just to showcase a ringer. He couldn't find anyone better for the band than the woman belting out "Misery Business" in front of them.

At the end of the song, she waited for Keon's cue to play a new one.

"Can you play," Tick looked down at the list Keon asked all the prospective talent to prepare, "'Drive'?"

"Sure." Clare winked.

Her fingers deftly picked the strings leading into a slower tune. The soft lyrics escaped her lips and pulled Spencer into a trance. The room disappeared. His focus existed only on her. Air caught in his throat when she looked at him, never shying away from looking directly into his eyes.

When the song ended, a jab to his side brought him back to the present. His cheeks burned as he avoided Keon's stare.

"Alright, Clare. We want to hear two other songs, but we want to hear how you perform with us. We'll play 'All Babes are Wolves' and then we'll play 'Least of My Kind.'"

She nodded her head with a smile and moved to change her setup to play with the group. Spencer felt Keon pat him on the shoulder. He swallowed hard. How would he be able to play while she sang next to him? With a shake of his head, he grabbed his guitar and checked the tuning, then plugged it into his amp.

Tick smiled wide at him, then nodded at Keon on the drums. Spencer nodded at Keon as well. Clare also gave her signal, then Keon started the song with a bang of the bass drum.

Spencer went into the song with no problem. Clare kept the rhythm and sang like she wrote the song herself. The full sound of her vocals warmed him to the core. He knew Keon and Tick would choose her as well, but he didn't want to seem too eager.

After the song ended, Keon's grin almost blinded Spencer. Tick also looked delighted with the outcome of how they performed together.

The last song would clinch the decision. Over a decade ago, "Least of My Kind" became a theme song for their pack, The Old Moss Pack, and now the band played it whenever they had a pack event, at least four times a year.

The original song by Echo's Children had a folk sound. They arranged it into a slow punk rock song. The lyrics were the critical part. A story about a wolf alone in a fight, only to hear their wolf family come to their aid as they lay dying. The song hit home for the pack and their history with hunters and death.

Spencer learned later that the writer wrote the song based on a character she played in a role-playing game. He never knew something like Dungeons and Dragons could inspire such an amazing song.

"That was great, Clare." Keon spun his sticks in his hands. "Are you ready for this last song?"

"Sure." She strummed her strings softly.

Keon nodded to Tick for the intro. They strummed the bass, sliding down the notes to hit a darker tone. Spencer and Clare joined in, and Keon played his drums with his hands, making it sound like a drum circle.

A haunting sound came out of Clare's mouth when she sang.

"Covered in dirt and mud, aching and spitting blood,
Cursing, you stir to rise and groan.
Muffled in yet-to-come mutters a battle drum
Werewolves don't usually walk alone."

Shivers flew down Spencer's spine as he played. He felt the wolf inside of him push forward more. No longer content to just watch Clare, he wanted to come forth and take over, to shift right there in the open garage. His breathing quickened. Wide-eyed, he looked over at Tick.

They visibly shook as they played. Their eyes twitched and darted to him, their wolf visible in their eyes.

Impossible, he thought. Tick wasn't born a werewolf, so they shouldn't be able to shift at will. Fur covered Keon's arms and his wolf shone brightly in his eyes, but he grinned from ear to ear and kept hitting the drums.

Spencer's heart pounded, but he continued playing as Clare sang. Her voice called to him. The lyrics called to his wolf, and apparently to the others as well. Sheer will kept his wolf at bay.

Soon the song slowed with the last lines,

"Better beware, my lord; better prepare, my lord;

I was the least of my kind."

Clare's voice held the last note longer than Dan's ever could. At the end Keon let off a growl. The wolf inside pulled back, content to sit and watch again. Keon's fur retreated before Clare could see. Tick put down their bass and walked inside the house.

"Is she okay?" Clare asked.

"They're fine." Keon walked over and shook Clare's hand. "Thank you for auditioning. That was great."

"Thanks. I had fun."

The smile she gave Keon caused a fire to burn in Spencer's eyes. He pulled back his desire to punch his friend and took a deep breath.

"We should have a decision by the end of the week. I'll call you either way."

"Sounds good. I look forward to hearing the results." She unplugged her guitar and pulled it off her shoulder.

Spencer quickly pulled his off as well and walked over to her.

"Need any help packing up?"

"Trying to get rid of me fast, huh?" She laughed.

"No. Just wanting to be nice." He rubbed the back of his neck with a sigh.

The Wolf's Song | 21

"I got it. Thanks, though." She secured the case and stood up.

"I can walk you to your car." He straightened his back, waiting for a reply. He could see the top of her head, so he slouched.

"I parked one house over, unless you think this is a dangerous neighborhood."

"Right. It was nice meeting you...Clare."

She smiled up at him. "Nice meeting you as well, Spencer."

The way she said his name melted him inside. She walked down the driveway toward her car. He watched from where he stood as she got in and drove away.

"What ya staring at?" Keon asked right into Spencer's ear.

Spencer jumped. "Do you have to do that?"

"Yes. And as much as I'd love to tease you right now, we need to check on Tick."

Spencer looked toward the door to the house. They left right after the song. The two of them ventured into Keon's house. Tick sat on the couch in the living room with their head between their knees. Keon sat across from them on the coffee table.

"What's wrong?"

"What was that?" Tick asked.

"What?" Keon raised an eyebrow.

"She sang that song and pulled at my wolf. I almost shifted in the garage." They sat up, still shaking. Their right eye twitched.

"That's weird. I felt my wolf come forward, but

nothing weird happened."

"Nothing weird happened?" Spencer hit Keon on the head. "You had fur growing out of your arms. All of our eyes changed."

Keon's eyes widened. "Really?"

"Yes, really." Tick shook their head. "This is serious. I love her sound. I love how she sounds with us. But something about her singing 'Least of My Kind' calls to our wolves. If, and I mean if, we decide that she's our new singer, then we won't be able to play that song as often. Like, never in mixed company."

Keon forced air out of his nose. "I like her. I think she fits with the band. Our fourth of Wolves on Fire. I vote yes."

Tick rubbed their face with their hands. The eye spasms slowed. "I've never felt my wolf pull on me outside of a full moon. If y'all agree to help me learn to counter that feeling and agree to not play 'Least of My Kind' outside of a pack event, I also vote yes."

Spencer smiled. "Yes. Even though Keon played us by having two crappy musicians audition before her."

"Great. I'm glad you appreciate what I do for this group. Now, we need to present her to Ethan to get approval to tell her about the supernatural and then tell her about, well, the supernatural."

"Well, Keon, since you're the new spokesperson for the band, I suppose you get to talk to Ethan." Tick patted his shoulder with a laugh.

"We don't need to talk to Ethan. We can just tell her. Or rather. I should tell her." Spencer took a deep breath.

"What?" Keon asked. "You take over the pack while we weren't looking? All hail Spence 'the wolfman' Luvel?"

"Was there a vote we missed?"

Spencer rolled his eyes. "No, morons. She's my mate."

His two friends and bandmates stood up.

"Really?" Tick asked.

He nodded. The two pulled him down into a hug. Tick jumped up and down with their arms wrapped around him.

They pulled back and pinched his cheeks. "I'm so happy for you."

"I'm no longer happy for me." He pushed Tick off. "You're hurting my face."

"Don't care." And they plopped back onto the couch. "What about Jen?"

"Oh yeah. Jen." Keon's eyes widened. "You'd better cut things off with her."

"She's dating someone else now. I've got nothing to worry about."

"I agree with Keon. You should let her know. She comes on really strong when she's in between boyfriends."

"I'll just set her up with you." Spencer patted Keon on the face.

Chapter 4

Spencer

Spencer walked to the back door of Maggie's expanded bungalow and knocked on the pale-yellow door. He imagined the sun faded the door over time. Maggie never shied away from bright colors.

He heard her call for him to open the door. He walked into the kitchen of the old house. To the left held the kitchen, a large island in the middle of a u-shaped counter complete with a stove, sink, dishwasher, and refrigerator. The island, installed in the last decade, added work space and storage.

He raised an eyebrow at Maggie. She worked at the counter, organizing small vials of various spells. He almost didn't recognize her.

"Your hair, it's brown," he walked over to her and leaned against the island.

"You learned your colors!" she kissed his cheek. "I'm so proud."

He smiled at her. "Thanks. It took a while, but

nothing gets past me. Who convinced you to dye it?"

"Emma. I don't think it will help, but on the off chance it does, I'd rather put up with her telling me 'I told you so' than being dead."

"I might rather be dead. Emma can be rather insufferable."

Maggie laughed. "I'll tell her."

"No, you won't. I have enough dirt on you for you to keep your mouth shut."

"Sure, you do."

Spencer winked at her and started helping with her instruction.

"Where am I taking all of this again?" The full box was almost ready to send.

Maggie made a werewolf antidote that Spencer transported to different packs across the southeast. The antidote only worked within the first 48 hours after a werewolf's bite. Over the last month and a half, the number of werewolves biting humans rose dramatically. He suspected the hunter group Cernunnos was behind the attacks.

"Macon. The Middle Georgia Pack, so it's a quick trip. You can stay with their leader, Selma, if you want."

"I like the Macon pack. They are very hospitable. They usually feed me as well."

Maggie placed a note inside the box and closed it. Before he could pick it up, the backdoor opened, and Clare walked in.

"Clare." He stood with his hands on the sides of the box.

"Spencer. What are you doing here?" She looked back and forth between him and Maggie.

"I agreed to deliver some… stuff for Maggie. What are you doing here?"

"I live here." She closed the door.

"You what?"

"She lives here while she finds a better place to stay. She moved in on short notice and I'm friends with her grandmother." Maggie frowned at him. "Spencer is Emma's brother."

"You're the roommate."

"I'm the roommate. And you're the brother."

"Yeah." He stared at her, his face slack, his mind blank.

"How often do you deliver stuff for Maggie?" Her head tilted to the side and the side of her lip tugged upward.

He felt himself sliding off the counter. Standing straight, he cleared his throat. "Like once a week at most. And only for … uh…"

His mind went blank. How did Maggie phrase it? He couldn't say, 'I only deliver werewolf antidotes to surrounding packs.'

"Only my most prominent customers or items that could get damaged during shipping." Maggie patted Spencer on the shoulder with a wink.

"Thanks again for letting me know the band picked me. I'm really excited. Keon emailed me the song list and some other stuff to get familiar with." Her smile gave him butterflies in his stomach.

"You were the best of the bunch. I think Keon purposely chose some other, less than qualified musicians because he liked your sound."

"I won't hold it against him. I am pretty great." She let out a warm laugh.

Under his breath, he said, "That you are." Stepping forward, he picked up the box for transport. "Did Keon tell you we have a performance next week?"

"He mentioned it in the email. I know a good portion of the songs on the list, so with a little hard work, it should be fine."

"Listen, do you want to get coffee sometime?"

She stilled, "Uh..."

"You can ask questions about the group and what a typical performance is like as well as what we do during practices." He reminded himself not to push or scare her away.

"Yeah. That would be nice. When will you be back?"

"I have to be back tomorrow morning. I'm working a blood drive at one of the schools, so any time after six should work."

"Okay. I'll be free then. Text me where to meet you. Anyway, I'll let you get on the road. Be careful."

She waved and walked out of the kitchen into the living room. He heard her footsteps on the stairs.

Spencer took a deep breath while clutching the box.

"If you grip that any tighter, you'll break some of the bottles." Maggie smirked at him, her dark brown hair limp around her face.

He eased his grip. "Sorry."

"Sorry? Is that all? That doesn't sound like something a member of the Luvel family would say." She placed her open hand on her chest, eyes wide and teasing.

"How about, wow, I hate your hair?"

"Me too. But you won't distract me from my real question. Is she...?"

"Yes. And I haven't told her, but I will. This is only the second time I've seen her."

"I wonder what her grandma will say?"

"Oh god, what if they hate me? I'm not exactly normal."

"You're normal enough. But that's not something you need to think about now. Ah, young love. Go deliver those potions. Save the worrying for me."

"You have enough to worry about."

"And that's exactly why I want to think about something else. I can't wait to dye my hair back."

"Alright. I'm going. If you see the real Maggie, tell her I said 'Hi.'" He darted out of the door before she could whack him.

~

Clare

Clare came back down the stairs after changing out of her work clothes. Spencer left soon after she went upstairs. She waved at Maggie as she walked out the back door toward the river.

Maggie's greenhouse took up half the backyard. It looked like a traditional greenhouse made of wood and glass. Bricks lined the bottom three feet of the walls. Inside, it contained a variety of plants most Clare didn't recognize. Maggie spent an hour on the weekdays and over three on weekends tending to the plants.

Clare peeked inside as she passed. Behind the glasshouse sat a lovely bench facing the river. Clare didn't stop at the bench. She preferred to sit on the grass as close to the river as she could without getting a wet bottom. The sound of the flowing river made her happy. This spot erased the stress of the day. Now she knew she couldn't live without a river or pond nearby.

Staring out over the few feet of marsh grass between her and the water, she found her thoughts drift to Spencer. His call that morning surprised her. She expected to hear from Keon, not Spencer. When she answered the phone, his voice sent shivers down her arms. Her heart skipped a beat when she saw him in Maggie's kitchen. He appeared flustered at first, but slipped into an easy smile. Why did he have to be so sexy? The way his hands gripped the box made her wonder what they would feel like on her skin.

She wrapped her arms around her legs. The warm sun started to set. She rubbed her arms, but not from the cold. Goosebumps popped up each time she thought of Spencer's face. Maybe things would work out. Her crush wouldn't last long. She didn't want to end her moment with the band before it started. Just because he happened to be her type didn't mean she would automatically date him. She had self-control.

She laughed at herself. Her lack of self-control is the

reason her parents compared her to her near perfect cousins. It also contributed to her last failed relationship and exit from the previous band. Of course, her last boyfriend didn't know how to be amicable. After they split, he caused problems for her at work and in the band. She told herself and her parents she didn't run away from the situation, but they all knew it was a lie.

Now she couldn't stop thinking of the lead guitar player of Wolves on Fire. She shook her head. She needed to focus on anything else. The red and pink sunset reflected off the river. In the distance, she watched the bugs dance over the water. The light hit them, causing them to shine in a multitude of colors. Savannah wasn't so bad, she reminded herself. She had a job, a place to stay, and now a sexy guitar player to watch.

Chapter 5

Clare

The day passed in a blur. No matter how much Clare reminded herself that it wasn't a date, her excitement of meeting Spencer after work buzzed through her.

She knew dating a bandmate could end poorly. As the last to join, she would be the first to go. Try as she might, since she laid eyes on him during her audition, he rarely left her thoughts. His brown eyes, shaggy hair, the tattoos peeking from the bottom of his t-shirt, and his voice all consumed her brain. She wanted to inspect his tattoos up close, and she wanted to hear him play again. The way he played the guitar impressed her greatly. She never imagined that a local band this good would still play small gigs. She understood playing for fun, but fun bands couldn't execute music like Wolves on Fire.

She shook her head and looked back at the file in front of her. She knew music wouldn't pay her bills, so she needed to concentrate on the job in front of her.

At 6:30, she stepped into Gallery Espresso in

downtown Savannah. She didn't have time to change before she set off for the cafe. The local coffee shop contained an impressive collection of art on the walls. Upon closer inspection, she noticed the 'for sale' tags on each one. She didn't see Spencer, so she went to the counter to order a coffee. Clare picked a table along the wall to sit, which gave her a full view of the cafe and all who entered.

Three minutes later, Spencer rushed through the door, looking left and right, panting. She raised her hand when he looked her way. Relief flashed over his face as he headed toward her table.

She admired his easy walk over to her and the way his slim jeans low on his hips looked. He hadn't shaved since the day before, and she spied a silver necklace that disappeared under his gray t-shirt.

"Sorry I'm late." He sat across from her with a sigh. "Clean up took longer than usual."

"It's no problem. I like this cafe. And the coffee is delicious." She took a sip, smiling into the cup. The soothing, dark brew kept her from grinning like an idiot.

"So do you have any specific questions or would you like me to ramble on about the band?" He lifted the corner of his mouth. She swore his eyes twinkled a bit.

"I have questions, but I kind of want to watch you ramble."

"You request the torture option, so be it."

She laughed and shook her head.

"It's not that bad. Unless you ask my sister, then she'll tell you different."

"Oh, now I'll ask her."

His eyebrows scrunched together, "How..."

"I've met her. Through Maggie."

"Right. I feel like an idiot."

"You also look like one." She laughed at her own joke. "I'm just kidding."

"You wound me. I guess we can't be friends." He frowned and stood.

"Oh, come on," she stared at him. "Are you really leaving?"

He grinned down at her. "Nah. I'm going to get some coffee. Want anything?"

"No, I'm good." She sat back and watched him disappear behind the small barrier between the seats and the counter.

He came back shortly with a black coffee.

"Now, where to begin?" He tapped his chin.

"Why don't you start by telling me about the members? I understand Keon is a mechanic?"

"Right." He took a sip of his coffee. "He's a mechanic. Works over at Massey and Sons. Great place to get car work done, if you need it. His dad works there too. Keon isn't always aware of his surroundings on stage. It could catch on fire and he'd keep playing. Totally different off stage, though. Very organized."

Clare nodded. Spencer sat back in his chair and looked up with a squint.

"Tick is non-binary and uses they/them pronouns. It took me a few months to stop using she/her pronouns. They work as a medical coder at one of the hospitals or for a company the hospital outsources to. I'm not sure which. It's not their favorite. Tick keeps talking about doing something different. They just haven't decided. Best bass player around, though. They can play all the songs with their eyes closed, even new ones. It's like they can feel the next note."

She watched him soften as he spoke about his bandmates. She hoped he'd do the same with her one day. "And you?"

He snapped his head back. "Me? I just do odds and ends."

"Odds and ends?" She frowned and raised an eyebrow. "Maggie said you're a phlebotomist and you courier her goods. Surely, she pays you."

"Yeah. I do all that. It never feels as important as what everyone else does. I guess I've been waiting for something."

His brown eyes peered into hers. Butterflies swarmed her stomach, warming her to her cheeks. She swallowed with a shaky breath. Time moved slowly, never blinking. Chills trickled up her spine. This confirmed her suspicion that Spencer was dangerous and delicious. And she knew she'd be hard pressed to walk away.

She shook her head and blinked, taking a moment to taste her lukewarm drink. "I'm impressed with your guitar skills."

"I practiced more than I like to let on. It has been a constant for me over the last decade."

"Well, it shows. I'm happy that you all chose me to be in your band."

"Y'all."

"What?"

"Y'all. You're in the south now. Might as well pick up the lingo."

She leaned forward. "I don't think that will happen."

"Why not?" He cocked his head to the side.

She admired the line that trailed from behind his jaw down past his Adam's apple. She cleared her throat. "It's hard to shake twenty years of learned vernacular. I think I'd rather hear it on your tongue than mine."

The left side of his mouth slowly rose into a perfect smirk. "Is that so? What else would you like to hear on my tongue?"

She leaned back with wide eyes. "Anyway, which songs do you play at every show?"

He laughed. "Whatever list Keon gave you is what we normally play. The favorites are 'Where is My Mind', 'Ain't No Rest for the Wicked', and 'I Write Sins Not Tragedies.'"

"That's good to know. I'll have to brush up on the last one."

"You'll do fine. If you can learn and play the three songs Keon gave you within two days, you're better than the rest of us."

"Do you think I could add songs to the playlist?"

"Yeah. We all vote on the songs we play. Has to be unanimous, unless someone is paying us lots of money to play a specific song."

"How often does that happen?" She put her elbow on the table and her head in her hand.

"Not as much as it used to. We used to play bar mitzvahs and sweet sixteen parties. After so many years, we never want to play certain songs ever again."

"Now I want to know what those songs are." She grinned and grabbed his hand. Goosebumps traveled up her arms, but she held fast. "Tell me."

"No. You'll use it against us. I can't tell." His other hand rested on top of hers.

She squeezed. "Please."

"You're dangerous. I think we misjudged you."

She took back her hand and gasped. "You wound me, sir."

He smiled at her theatrics. "What about you? You now know a little about us. What's your story? How did you end up at Maggie's?"

"I'm a mechanical engineer. I worked in Pennsylvania, but wanted to work somewhere different. After applying to several places, I got a job here in aviation, but they needed me to start immediately. My ammachi knows Maggie and asked for a favor. I hope I can move out in another month or two. I'm on a few apartment waiting lists. I'm sure Maggie wants her house back."

"Ammachi? Your grandmother?"

Clare nodded.

"Since she's friends with Maggie, does she practice the witchy arts as well? I mean, that's what Maggie sells."

"I don't know. She never talks about her past or beliefs. My appachin, or grandfather, is Christian, as is my dad. My mom and her family are Hindus. I noticed when

I was younger that my ammachi never said any of the prayers in church, but I never asked her about it. Now I don't know if I want to know."

"And what are you?"

"Nothing, I suppose. Or agnostic? I find religion interesting, but my parents never forced me to pick a side. I guess it's just easier to hope there's a God or Gods without being specific as to which ones. What about you, Mr. Nosey?"

"I believe in the earth, the moon, and the sun. I'll also tell people I'm a heretic if I don't like them." His eyes lit up, and he smirked.

"Charming. I'm sure that goes over well here in the south."

"The reactions are amusing."

Imagining the faces of stunned little old ladies caused Clare to laugh. "How often do you tell people that?"

"Not as often as I'd like."

She shook her head and finished her drink. "You're a bad influence. One more question before I go. How do you all dress when performing? Do you wear whatever you want? Keep a punk vibe? Pastels to throw people off?"

He laughed, filling her stomach with flutters. "We try to keep a punk vibe, but that doesn't mean you can't stick to something plain. It gets hot in the summer. Sometimes shorts and a t-shirt are best."

"Great. Thanks for meeting me." She stood and grabbed her bag. "I should get going. I'm sure you're exhausted from driving so much and then working all day."

"Actually, I'm starving. Are you hungry? There's a great sandwich shop about a block from here."

"Sandwich shop?" She frowned.

"It's South African inspired."

She paused for a few seconds. "I'm in. I love trying new foods." Clare knew she should say no. Spending more time with Spencer alone could end in disaster. Just like before.

~

Spencer

Spencer looked over at Clare as they walked toward Zunzi's. The wind waved her black hair around the shoulders of her yellow blouse. He liked her work attire, yet he couldn't help but want to see her dressed down again. Seeing her in jeans with her guitar draped across her became an instant fantasy.

He hoped she liked their sandwiches. If she liked it, she might stay longer. Every little bit he learned about her would bring them closer together.

"So Zunzi's is South African inspired?" she smiled his way.

They could see the sign up ahead and all the large rainbow umbrellas on the patio.

"Yeah. I don't know how authentic it is, but I'd definitely go to South Africa-based on this place alone." Her laugh brought a smile to his face.

"Where wouldn't you visit based on the food you've

eaten in this very American city?"

"Um…" he pondered the question. He enjoyed most food. "The land of Emma."

"Emma can't cook?"

"No. It's terrible. She's the reason I learned to cook. Our dad cooked. I cooked. She made spaghetti and tacos. They were at least edible."

Clare held onto his shoulder while she giggled. "That's fantastic. So does your dad live here, too?"

He frowned. For a moment, pain gripped his chest. "He did. He passed away a few years ago."

She stopped walking. Her chin met her sternum. "Oh. I'm sorry to hear that. I didn't mean to bring up such a sad subject."

He paused long enough to grab her hand and pull her next to him. Then kept walking, not letting go of her. "I have only happy memories of my dad. You didn't do anything wrong."

She glanced up at him. Her dark eyes brightened. "So, what do you suggest I try?"

"Honestly, you can't go wrong with anything, so try what sounds good to you." He stopped in front of the door and stood in line. She glanced through the menu while he tried to follow her eyes to see what interested her.

"What do you think you'll get?" His voice came out in a whisper.

"My instinct is to go with the Rising Sun, but I can't pass up a sandwich called Booty Roll." Her smile reached ear to ear when she looked at him. "You?"

"I'm going to get a Bird Island."

"Nice call."

They sat at a table outside under one of the rainbow umbrellas. He watched her eyes roll back into her head as she took her first bite.

"This is so good. Thank you for bringing me here."

"Of course. I'll make sure you try all the best places around here."

He picked at his food, too busy watching her take bite after bite. He wanted to be the reason her eyes rolled back in her head. She tilted her head each time she took a bite, exposing her neck. He could reach out and touch it, touch her. His hand still tingled from where he held her hand.

She looked at him and raised an eyebrow. "Wha?" she asked with a full mouth.

He laughed. "That good, huh?"

She swallowed her food. "Of course."

"I'm glad," he said with a wink.

"So, we have a long practice on Saturday. What's that like?"

"Long." He watched her long fingers place a fry into her mouth. "Keon has us all play through the songs we know. We discuss which songs to put into the next set and in what order. Then we play those songs in that order. After that we go through the parts that aren't so smooth. It might be longer than usual, since it's your first practice."

"Do we get to eat sometime in there?" She frowned, a fry mere inches from her mouth.

"Yes. We all bring something to share. We take regular breaks. He is gracious and lets us pee when we need to, like adults."

She chuckled. "I vaguely remember reading that food part. I've been so worried about the music. Each night I go over the songs he gave me. I have most of them down. Of course, it will be different when we play together."

"I can't wait." He leaned toward her, his heart pumping.

"Me either."

A bell rang on her phone. She pulled it out. "Oh. That's my parents. They want me to call. And it's getting late."

She wrapped up the rest of her food and threw the trash away. He hastily followed her lead.

At the door, she turned to him. "I'll see you tomorrow?"

"Yes." He opened the door for her. "I'll walk you to your car."

"Okay."

He walked with her across the street. She stopped at the second car down. "Thanks for seeing me safely to my car." She laughed and opened the door.

He leaned over and kissed her cheek. "I'll see you tomorrow."

He pivoted away and walked down the street, not looking back, though he desperately wanted to. Once he reached the corner, he turned to see her drive off. With his back against the building at the end of the block, he breathed out a heavy sigh. He didn't tell her. He couldn't.

She'd run. And he'd break.

Chapter 6

Spencer

Spencer walked up to Keon's half raised garage door, guitar in hand. He bent from the waist and moved inside the garage. Keon sat at the drums, playing the air with his sticks. His closed eyes and bobbing head told Spencer all he needed to know. The music played in his head. Keon's mohawk of tight black curls bobbed back and forth to the music inside his mind. He called his hairstyle a mohawk fade. Spencer just wanted to know why he hadn't dyed it yet.

Tick walked into the garage from inside the house. They balanced an apple and a glass of water in one hand to open the door. The shortest group member until Clare came along, Tick played bass. They kept their hair short and colorful. It'd been blue for the last few months. They loved to play, but hated being the center of attention. They did what they could to stay out of the spotlight on stage. Honestly, the band couldn't do this without them.

Of course, Spencer thought that about the entire

group until Dan left. And now they found out that Dan could be replaced. Would it be the same with all of them?

"So, lover boy," Tick said, "you tell her yet?"

He sighed and shook his head. "Not yet."

"Don't wait too long. I don't want to get attached just to watch her leave because of your dumbass."

"I can feel the love." Spencer leaned his guitar against the wall and headed to take his bag of banana bread and snickerdoodles into Keon's kitchen.

"You gotta tell her within the week. We have a pack party to play at, and I want her to feel comfortable around all the wolves." Keon didn't even open his eyes when he spoke.

Spencer held his breath and continued into the kitchen. He placed the containers beside the tray of half-sliced fruits and vegetables. Tick. Someone must have convinced them they could cut up everything themselves, then got bored with the task. Spencer didn't blame them, though he'll probably finish the job later.

The door opened from the garage, and a flash of black hair floated through. Spencer looked up to see Clare smiling at him with two small pans stacked in her arms. She walked over and placed them next to him.

"Oh, what'd you bring?" She lifted the top of his container. "Are those cookies?"

"Yeah. Snickerdoodles."

"I love snickerdoodles. Did you make them?"

"Yeah." He smiled. Her eyes widened.

"You cook, you bake, play guitar, and draw blood. What can't you do?"

"I can think of a few things." He blinked back his anxiety about telling her the truth. "What did you bring?"

"Plain white rice and Puliyogare, which is a tangy-spicy rice. Keon said he had pulled pork, so I thought the rice would go well."

"I look forward to the puliyogare."

"You said it right. I hope you like it." She turned and put her items in the fridge. "Come on."

She grabbed his hand and pulled him into the garage. He wanted to pull her back, wrap his arms around her, stick his face into the crook of her neck, and breathe her in. Instead, he followed her, knowing that he'd follow her anywhere.

~

Clare

The song ended, and Clare instinctually turned toward Keon. He gave his thoughts after each piece instead of waiting for the end. She stood with her guitar hung off her shoulder, breath held in her chest, and waited. It was the last song on the list. Clare wondered if she'd improved after receiving critiques over the last twenty-ish songs.

Keon leaned over the drum set and smiled up at them. "That was great. The only thing I'd change is to let Spencer come in with the chorus while you finish the verse, then you can follow through. You two sing well together. I never thought I'd say this, but I think we could pull off that Arctic Monkeys' song, 'Do I Wanna Know.'

Spencer, you and Dan couldn't quite get the timing right, but I think you can pull it off with Clare." He sat back and tossed a drumstick, catching it with ease.

"Break time?" Tick asked.

They hadn't said much, but the bass player looked pleased. Well, they looked pleased to Clare.

"Break time." Keon nodded at Tick, stepping over his throne.

Clare pulled her guitar over her shoulder and placed it on the stand she brought for it. She looked up in time to feel Spencer tug her elbow toward the door to the house. He smiled back at her, then paused, waving her through first.

Keon and Tick stood in the kitchen with their hands in the bowl of snickerdoodles. Tick picked up the container when they walked up. "This is mine. You can't have any."

Clare laughed. "I'm not even going to try. I have a feeling you'll take my hand off."

Tick smiled at her, showing all their teeth with a growl. Spencer slapped their arm.

"Should I be worried?" Clare asked Spencer.

"Nah," he said. "They just like sweets. I can make you some more if you want to try them."

"Just don't tell Tick about it if you do."

"You brought rice, right?" Keon asked, rummaging in the fridge.

"Yeah. It's the two covered in foil."

He pulled them out and uncovered the dishes. "OH, these look good. This one spicy?"

"A little. I tried to tone it down."

"I have a spicy friend." He put a large spoonful on his plate next to the pulled pork.

"Excuse me?" Spencer put a hand on Keon's arm. "What do you mean, 'spicy friend'?"

"Spicy food. Y'all don't like the spice. Y'all get mad when I add hot sauce. It's a new era, the era of flavor."

Clare grinned at Spencer's reddening cheeks. "Are you embarrassed?"

He wouldn't meet her eyes. "No. I'm sure it's not that spicy. As long as it doesn't sear off my taste buds, I'm okay. Keon seems to think anything less than nuclear is bland."

"I think Keon and I need to have a little competition some time."

She glanced at Spencer as he put a spoon full of her dish on his plate. "What's this called again?"

"Puliyogare. My mom used to make it all the time."

His soft smile froze her on the spot. Those brown eyes searched hers. She wanted to know what he was looking for, why he looked at her that way. His hand lightly touched her arm as he leaned toward her.

"You smell amazing."

His whisper sent goosebumps down her body. She held her breath.

"Y'all gonna stand in the kitchen all day? We've got a set list to make." Keon's voice caused Clare to jump.

With a quick smile at Spencer, she cut in and made her own plate. She settled on the couch while Tick and Keon took the two single recliners in the room. Spencer slowly followed and sat right beside Clare. She looked down at his leg, almost touching hers, on the three-seat sofa. She took a bite of her food and ignored the way both Keon and Tick shook their heads at her and Spencer.

"Our next gig is Thursday. We'll introduce Clare as our new vocalist. Any thoughts on what to start with?" Keon placed his now empty plate on the coffee table.

"I think we should start with a strong song and end with a strong song." Tick stood and handed Clare a snickerdoodle.

"Thanks. I think that's smart. I want to give a good first impression." Clare smelled the cookie before taking a bite. Cinnamon. Spencer kind of smelled like cinnamon. And ginger and sweat. She shivered.

"You okay?" Spencer asked.

He didn't touch her, yet his voice blanketed her in desire. She knew this was a bad plan. And he sat too close to her.

She focused on Keon, never turning her eyes on Spencer. "Yeah. How many songs do you play in a set again? We can go down the list and eliminate my weakest songs, building the set from what's left."

"You don't have many that I'd call weak. We can all call out a song we don't want to play on Thursday, no questions asked, and move on from there." Keon grabbed a notebook and pen from the coffee table.

Clare noticed a light brushing of her hip as they talked through the order of what songs they considered definites and maybes. She didn't look, but she knew. Spencer's thumb rubbed up and down the side of her shirt, his arm behind her. With a quick glance his way, it didn't appear that he realized his own actions.

The constant movement of his thumb raised her shirt, and he grazed the skin. She stood when she felt the skin-on-skin contact, to the surprise of the rest of the group.

"I'll start cleaning up. You can keep talking."

She gathered up as many dishes as she could carry and brought them into the kitchen. At the sink, she took a deep, shaky breath. Why did Spencer put his arm around her? And why did it light a fire within her when he touched her skin?

She threw away the paper products and put the other dishes into the dishwasher.

Keon talked to her while she worked. The desire to turn and look at Spencer overwhelmed her. She could feel his eyes on the back of her head. Or that's what she imagined.

"Sure," she answered without knowing what he said.

She couldn't get involved with Spencer. The situation reminded her too much of her last disaster of a relationship. Plus, she really wanted to stay in the band. Even after just half a day, she felt like she belonged. Giving into her lust for Spencer would ruin everything.

After more murmuring among the group in the living room, another question came her way.

"Sounds good." A lump stuck in her throat. She really shouldn't answer questions she didn't hear.

After a few deep breaths, she rejoined the group.

"How do you feel about ending on 'Misery

Business'?" Keon looked up as she entered the room.

"That sounds good. Can I see the order again?"

He handed her the list. Half her brain took in the order, nodding in approval. The other half took peeks at Spencer, still on the couch, leaned forward with elbows on his knees, and eyes focused on her.

"The only one on the list I'd like to practice the most is 'I want to be Sedated.'"

"We'll go through the entire list in a few, then on Tuesday we'll practice the ones we feel the least comfortable with." He took the list from her hands.

Clare gathered the rest of the dishes and carried them to the kitchen. It gave her a second chance to catch her breath. She didn't know if she had it in her to ignore Spencer in this setting. She looked up and found his eyes trained on her. She didn't look away, but let her heart beat faster from the attention. He was a captivating man, and she didn't stand a chance.

~

Spencer

With the set list created, the band moved back to the garage. Spencer picked up his guitar, checking the strings, the cables, and the amp. No matter how often he played in a day, he always checked his gear after a break. He learned that the hard way years ago right before a gig. Somewhere between the sound check and the concert, the wire from the guitar to his amp stopped working, and it delayed the concert by fifteen minutes while they fixed the situation.

He looked up to see Clare watching him. The incident on the couch came to mind, and he kicked himself when he realized why she moved so fast. How or when his arm snaked around her, he didn't know. Self-sabotage was real.

"A professional. You always check your gear before you play?" Clare strummed her instrument, then plugged in the amp.

"Yeah. I've been burned in the past, so now I always check. You?"

"Yep, but only because someone ingrained it in me. He must have been a boy scout."

Spencer listened to her laugh at her own words. The sound settled his anxiety.

"Do you all have any original songs?"

"A few. I think Keon wanted to get you comfortable before we gave you something completely new. I'm sure you'll get it soon, though."

"You know, I kind of like that the drummer is in charge. It's a nice change of pace." She looked back at Keon for a second.

Spencer's eyes didn't falter from her face. Her short hair fell forward, covering one of her eyes. He longed to tuck it behind her ear, then kiss her senseless.

His pants started to feel a bit tight. He looked away, but his wolf grumbled in his ear. When did his wolf decide to come forward?

"Hey, Spencer."

He heard his wolf huff and disappear into the back of

his mind. He didn't even need to look up to know Emma was there.

"We're rehearsing." He looked up at his sister walking across Keon's lawn with a bag draped over her shoulder behind her back. "Come back later."

"I know. That's why I'm coming to you. It will only take about twenty minutes if Keon will spare you for that long."

The bag rolled off her shoulder and swung from her hand beside her legs. He swallowed hard, heat rising under his collar.

"No. It's too soon."

The red bag, his red duffle bag, weighed around forty pounds. Emma held it like she would any small hand bag. It contained everything he needed to take blood, specifically from Emma. Her blood held the key to the werewolf antidote. If taken within 48 hours after a werewolf's bite, the person would not change. He knew the hunters were attacking various areas across the southeast. He'd transported enough of the potion within the last three weeks that he held little doubt Maggie's supply was running low. But it was too soon. He took over a pint last Saturday. She wasn't strong enough yet. There wasn't enough time for her body to replenish the blood supply, even if she were part wolf.

"It can't wait." She stood in front of him.

All eyes watched them stare each other down.

"No. It's. Too. Soon." He felt his lips pull tight; his eyes bored into his sister's.

"Too. Damn. Bad. It's needed." She broke eye

contact, looking behind him. "Mind if we borrow your spare bedroom?"

"Uh…" Keon said. "Sure?"

Spencer spun his head, giving his friend a death stare. Emma stepped lightly around the group and through the door leading into the house.

"Really?" he said to Keon.

"Yeah. I'm not crossing Emma." He held up his hands, surrendering to the situation.

"Dude. You gotta go." Tick plucked at the bass strings. "Some things are too important."

His nostrils flared as he put his guitar on its stand. Keon and Tick frowned at him, heads down, eyes only flickering toward him. Spencer turned to see Clare stared at him, her brows bunched over her eyes. Questions he could almost hear rolled off her in waves.

He walked past them all. "She's my sister." The door slammed behind him.

Emma stood next to the bed in Keon's spare room. She unloaded the bag of the supplies needed to draw blood, blood which Maggie needed to make the antidote.

She set the vial stand on the bedside table and filled it with empty vials. Beside it, she placed a set of needles, the tourniquet, alcohol wipes, and gloves. He washed his hands before he came into the room.

He sighed. "It's too dangerous, Em. It's too much. We took extra last week."

She looked up with a frown. "I don't have a choice. Maggie sent out all her supply this week. The hunters are getting bolder, and it's affecting packs in and out of our alliance."

"You're going to pass out. How are you getting this back to Maggie if you can't drive? How will you go to work if you're too weak to function?"

"I'll be fine."

"How many iron-rich foods have you eaten this week?" He stepped forward, placed two fingers on her neck, and felt her pulse. While her heartbeat appeared strong, the flow of blood felt light. He could always tell when a donor wouldn't pass the hemoglobin test for blood donation. Emma wouldn't pass.

"Enough." She pushed his hand away.

"It's not. I know Maggie didn't ask you to do this."

Her head dropped. "No, she didn't. She wouldn't. But I can't sit by and not help. I don't care how mad she'll be when I show up with vials in hand. It's the best thing about being a werewolf carrier."

"It's the worst thing. You're my sister. You're all I have, and you knowingly put yourself at risk all the time."

She squeezed his hand with a smile. "If I pass out, you can tell me 'I told you so' for as long as you like."

"No deal. I'll do it, but I'm going to monitor your eating for the next two weeks. You're needed for more than your blood."

With a salute, she climbed into the bed and laid back.

He put his gloves on and put the tourniquet on her arm. Taking Emma's blood was almost second nature to him. He could probably stick her without feeling for a vein at his point, but he checked anyway. After inserting the needle, he watched her face as he filled vial after vial, slowly loading up the small wire rack. When Spencer took nearly half a pint, her face paled, and her eyes couldn't stay open. In one quick step, he placed a gauze over the top of the needle, pulled it out, and pressed gauze over the puncture.

"We're not done."

"Yes, we are. You're about to faint."

"But…"

"No buts. You're just as important as the people you're trying to protect. Now hold this gauze down while I grab a bandage."

"Do you have green?"

She sounded weak. He worried he had taken too much. "Yeah. Here." He wrapped the green cohesive bandage over the gauze she held.

"Let me clean this up, and then I'll get you something to eat and drink."

She reached out and grabbed his wrist. "Thanks, Spencer."

He smiled down at her. In times like these, it seemed odd that he took care of her. She always watched over him. The perfect big sister.

"Well, I'm calling you if Maggie tries to kill me for this."

Chapter 7

Clare

"So...what was that about?" Clare looked back and forth between Tick and Keon.

"Nothing."

"Ah, the sibling argument was nothing." She turned to Tick. "Anything you want to share?"

"It's not for me to share." Tick frowned at her and shrugged.

"They're right. It's Spencer's job to tell you." Keon hit his stick on the side of his snare. "And it will be soon, or I'll kick his ass."

"Lovely." She looked down at her watch. "25 minutes. I have to pee."

"Go. Then see how much longer he'll be." Keon waved her toward the door.

She darted inside. She'd been holding it for fifteen minutes, but she didn't want to intrude, not that using the bathroom was intruding, but it might make them uncomfortable.

After washing her hands, Clare walked down the hall and peeked into the room at the end. Through the open door, she could see it must be Keon's. It looked like a room well lived in, with the comforter almost off the bed, clothes piled in the corner, and an electronic drum set.

She turned around and went to the only other door. She knocked, then turned the knob.

"Hey, how much longer are you going to be?"

The sparsely furnished room had a small bedside table, a dresser, and a bed that held the red duffle bag and Emma. "Hey, Clare," Emma said. "He's getting me something to eat."

"Are you okay?" She walked over to her and sat on the bed beside her.

"Yeah. Just a little weak." She grabbed Clare's hand and squeezed.

The squeeze felt strong to Clare, but Emma's face looked like ash and her body limp.

"Can you sing for me?" She smiled.

"Yeah. I can sing until Spencer gets back. What do you want to hear?"

"Have they taught you 'Least of My Kind' yet?"

"Yeah."

Emma's head rocked to the side to look straight at Clare. "Sing the chorus."

Clare nodded. Her thumb rubbed the back of Emma's hand as she began to sing softly,

"Think on the battle-cost; this time the wolf has lost
Beaten and broken and blind.
Better beware, my lord; better prepare, my lord;

I was the least of my kind."

Emma's grip on Clare's hand tightened with each line. Color flushed her cheeks, and her eyes grew wide.

"Stop," Emma cried.

Clare shut her mouth. *What happened*, she thought. "That bad, huh?" She tried to laugh at her own joke, but it sounded false.

"No. It was wonderful." Emma let go of Clare's hand. "Too wonderful."

She whispered the last part, but Clare still heard. Emma wouldn't meet her eyes, but sat straight up.

"You should probably stay lying down." Clare put her hand on Emma's shoulder, but her soft shove didn't even rock Emma from her position.

"Em, I have a plate for you and... Clare. What are you doing?" Spencer stood in the doorway, a plate of food in one hand and a large cup in the other.

"I came to see what was taking so long. Emma asked me to sit with her."

"Oh." He moved closer and handed Emma her food.

"You look better than you did five minutes ago."

"Clare sang for me."

Clare still couldn't get Emma to look at her. As much as she wanted to ask why, it sounded like a weird question, even in her head.

"I'll just go. I hope you feel better."

She stood and walked around Spencer. He reached out and held her wrist, keeping her in the room. With one look at him, her heart stopped. His expression looked raw with worry and stress. An urge to take him into her arms and protect him overcame her, but she couldn't move. Dangerous. *He's going to break my heart,* she thought.

"I'll be out in another five minutes, okay?"

She nodded, unable to speak. When she walked out to the garage, the feel of his grip burned around her wrist.

It took ten minutes for Emma to leave the house and for the group to continue rehearsal. The band's energy didn't reach the same level as the morning.

As they played through the set list, Keon rarely offered any feedback. Tick shrugged with a frown every time Clare looked at her, and Spencer didn't look her way at all. A massive elephant sat in the room. But she did not know what it was, only that it stifled their connection.

After they finished the last song in the set, Keon tucked his sticks away and walked toward the rest of them. "Let's practice for an hour tomorrow, Monday, and Tuesday. We'll rest on Wednesday. Anyone opposed to that?" He looked at each one in turn, his light brown eyes tired, a frown on his face.

No one spoke out against that plan, so he sent them inside to pick up their food and leave. Clare made her way to the kitchen, aware that no one followed her. They were keeping something from her.

Holding her dishes, she headed back out to the garage. Their whispers stopped when she opened the door.

Her face always showed her feelings and nothing she could do could stop it. Though she didn't want to say anything. They'd known each other for a week. They didn't have to tell her anything. If only she could be sure she wasn't the problem.

Minutes later, she picked up her equipment and food. "Great practice, everyone. See you tomorrow."

She lifted the food dishes in her hand, gave a wave, and walked down the driveway. She hoped the group's energy evened out by the next day, or at least by the gig on Thursday.

She heard her name as she opened her car door.

Spencer ran up with his head hung low. "I'm sorry. It really has nothing to do with you. It's just complicated and not something we really talk about with many people. But I promise, I'll tell you everything. Just…"

"Not now?" She raised an eyebrow with a smile, then started loading her car. "You don't have to tell me at all. I understand that you have known each other for…probably more than a decade. And you've just met me. Why would you want to tell me a secret, especially if it concerns your sister?"

His eyes searched hers like he could see inside her. She felt exposed in his gaze. A moment later, he wrapped his arms around her in a hug.

"Thank you," he said in her ear. "You really are amazing."

Pulling back, he placed his hand on her cheek. His warmth seeped into her. Before she could lean into his hand, it was gone.

"I'll see you tomorrow." He walked away with a wave.

She stood staring after him with only the food left in her hands. The feel of him pressed against her tingled over her body. Damn, those jeans fit him just right. She looked away before she dropped the food. Playing in the band with Spencer tested her restraint. She couldn't fall for him. He'd absolutely destroy her.

~

Emma

Maggie ground the ingredients with the mortar and pestle while watching Emma through squinted eyes. Emma worried the mortar would break as Maggie took her anger out on the herbs.

"I'm sorry," Emma said. Again. She sat in a chair against the back wall of the workshop, lacking the energy to move.

Maggie narrowed her eyes further, then turned away to add the powdered material to the large cauldron. She placed each spell ingredient in one at a time with a glare at Emma every few minutes. Once she added the last item to the pot, she turned on the burner underneath.

She cleaned up the workbench, slamming items into place. The sound echoed in the small room. Emma tried to appear small against the back wall by crossing her arms and legs and hunching over. She'd never seen Maggie like this, and they'd known each other for decades.

Maggie walked back to the cauldron and held her hand over the top. She whispered the spell over the bubbling concoction. Emma knew it by heart. She'd watched Gigi and Maggie make it almost as long as she'd known Maggie. When Emma was around seven years old, her father figured out that she was a carrier. She frowned, pushing the incident out of her mind.

A chair clunked onto the floor in front of her. She jumped. Maggie sat in front of her. Dark brown hair hung around her ears. It didn't match her. She looked like a completely different person. Even after four days, Emma wasn't used to the new look.

"Do you know how dangerous that was?" Maggie stared at Emma, her body shaking, her lips tight. "I can't believe Spencer agreed to it. I can't believe you thought it was a good idea. I will never forgive you if you die because you think we need more antidotes on the shelf."

She clenched her fist. "You are more than just a carrier. You don't owe the werewolf world anything. You don't need to overcompensate because you can't shift."

"I'm not overcompensating for anything." Emma unfurled herself, her back straight in the chair. "People need this. I want to help, and I can help. And I'll do it next week if I have to."

"Son of a bitch. Do you hear yourself? You can't help anyone if you don't take care of yourself." She rubbed her face with her hands. "Did Spencer at least give you a list of foods that are high in iron?"

"Yeah. He said to take a multivitamin and to eat and drink things with vitamin C and to avoid tea with my meals, as it hurts iron absorption."

Maggie grabbed Emma's hand. "You're my best friend. My lifeline. Please take care of yourself."

"Says the woman who refuses to let anyone protect her."

She rolled her eyes while waving her hand dismissively.

"But I do want to talk to you about one thing." Emma leaned forward. "Clare. What do you know about her?"

"I've told you everything I know about her. Why?"

"When I was lying on the bed, she came in and sat with me for a bit. I asked her to sing. Her voice, her song, pulled at the wolf inside of me. It gave me strength. I thought I would shift right there, and it scared me. I made her stop."

Maggie's eyes grew wide. "I don't know. Did you ask Spencer about it?"

"Yeah. He said he feels the same way when she sings 'Least of My Kind.'"

"Was that the song she sang for you?"

"Yeah," Emma whispered.

"And he doesn't feel the same way with any other song?"

"Right."

"Okay, so probably not all songs. Maybe because you and Spencer have such a strong connection to the song. That can be dangerous for the pack."

"We need to figure out how she does it. What she is."

"You mean beyond your future sister-in-law? Isn't that enough info for you?" Maggie gave her a weak smile.

"Exactly. If she's going to be family, I want to know what we're getting into."

Chapter 8

Spencer

Spencer jogged up to Keon's house the next day. Ten minutes late. He couldn't remember the last time he arrived to practice late.

"There he is," Keon called. "It's not like you to be late."

"Fighting with Emma." He opened his case and pulled out his guitar.

"How is she feeling?" Tick asked, using their deepest voice through the microphone set up for Clare.

Clare kneeled next to an amp, checking wires. She looked up at him through her lashes.

"She's feeling better. She doesn't like that I'm trying to get her to eat an iron-rich diet. She threw the iron pills I bought at my head." He shook his head. "She's a vet. She should know better."

"She probably does and thinks you're being patronizing." Clare stood with a frown.

"I hope that's it." He ran his hands through his hair

and tried not to stare at Clare. "I just want her to take care of herself. She stretches herself thin caring for others."

"Mamma Emma," Tick mumbled. "Always available to help."

Clare's expression softened at Tick's words. She placed a hand on their shoulder and moved to stand in front of the mic. Tick picked up their bass and got into position.

"I hope Emma takes it easy this week. Also, thanks for setting up without me yelling at you." Keon started a drumroll on his cymbal.

His eyes sparkled when he sat at his drum set. He'd always been the driver behind the band, even when Dan was officially in charge, and Spencer couldn't imagine having a band without him. Spencer checked all his equipment while Clare and Tick tuned their instruments. Five minutes later, they began.

Clare played and sang with half-closed eyes. Spencer smiled, seeing her shoulders relax the more they played. A bright smile lingered on Tick's face and Keon's wolf could be seen in his eyes. Spencer's wolf sighed each time he looked toward Clare. Warmth spread through his body. Here in Keon's garage, Spencer felt at peace. He hadn't felt this way for months.

After practice, he gathered up his gear and followed Clare without a goodbye to the others.

"Clare," he called. She looked back, but didn't stop. "You wanna go get some ice cream?" He caught up and moved in line with her.

"Who else is coming?" She stopped at her car and put everything inside.

"Just me. And you, if you want."

She side-eyed him. His heart beat faster. "You know, Tick said I should give you a chance."

"Yeah?" He held his breath.

"Yeah." Her eyes scanned his body, arms crossed over her chest. "I could go for ice cream."

"I'll drive." He used his head to point toward his car.

She locked her car and fell into step beside him. "My car better be safe here."

"It's safer here than downtown."

"Are we going downtown?"

"Of course. That's where the best ice cream is." He winked at her and she looked away.

He thought he saw her cheeks flush, but it might be the sun. Either way, he couldn't stop hoping she'd reacted to him.

~

Clare

The easy conversation between Spencer and Clare helped her relax as he drove. She glanced his way so many times she wasn't quite sure where they were.

His brown hair hung in his eyes, forcing him to brush it back with his hand at random intervals. A peaceful smile stayed on his lips as they traveled. She heard the flirtatious tone in his voice as they talked.

She thought back to what Tick told her. "Spencer is a

casual guy. I've never seen him actually pursue anyone. It means he's serious."

"What makes you think he's pursuing me?" Clare asked.

"The way he looks at you, how he's always a little too close. And he's asked us to give him advice on how to ask you out for the last two days. He called me at 11 last night. Give him a chance."

The situation looked the same as before, though. Girl dates guy in the same band, girl and boy fight, they break up. Guy makes life miserable for girl.

She appreciated how up front he acted with her. Somehow, she couldn't see Spencer actively making her life miserable.

Against the worried voice in her head, she followed Tick's advice. Of course, she questioned whether she should take advice from someone called Tick. They were a great bass player, though.

Sitting in the car, she got a detailed view of his profile. His soft, round chin contrasted against his pointed nose, and it gave her the urge to boop it or kiss it. She looked away before she could act on the impulse.

Spencer parked on a square, which one, she couldn't say, and they walked a few blocks until they stood in front of a shop called 'Leopold's Ice Cream.' Bright neon letters lit up the name on the front. She stopped to gaze up at the sign. Spencer pulled her toward the back of the long line, which spilled out the front door onto the sidewalk.

"Leopold's is the best ice cream in the city. Though some think River Street Sweets or Savannah Candy

Kitchen is better, they just don't know what they're talking about." He obviously believed it, based on the stern look on his face.

"I'll have to try all three and let you know what I think."

"You'll find the best and most interesting flavors here. They have the traditional ones, but they also create different flavors for each season, like peach, Girl Scout cookie ones, pumpkin spice, blueberry, oh, and rose petal cream. So good. Subtle flavor, light, refreshing."

Clare swore she saw stars in his eyes when he talked about the rose petal cream. "So, you just kind of like ice cream?"

"Yeah. It's okay." He let go of her hand and put them in his pockets. "I just come here once a week."

"Wow. That's a lot of ice cream. Are you ruined for store bought now?"

"Pretty much. I'll tolerate Talenti. I do like Jeni's and if I'm lucky and decide to go to the fancy grocery store, I can find Graeter's."

"Graeter's. Why does that sound familiar?"

"It's an ice cream shop out of Cincinnati."

She turned and grabbed his arm. "Oh, are you familiar with Cincinnati?"

"I'm familiar with the Ohio River." He grimaced.

"Really? Have you seen Foxy Shazam? They have one of the best performances."

"Oh yeah. They are amazing. Who do you love to watch live?"

"I had the chance to see Prince perform a few years

ago and it really blew me away."

"He came to Savannah, but I couldn't get tickets. Or afford tickets at that time."

"My dad's a huge fan, so I got lucky."

"Look, we can see the counter now."

Clare hardly noticed as they followed the dwindling line into the store.

"I'm going to get my favorite flavor as a test before I dip my toes into something new."

"Oh, and what's your favorite?"

"You'll see." She smiled at him and walked to the counter. Her face hung an inch away from the glass as she looked at all the flavors. She looked over to find Spencer watching her. He smiled.

"What?"

"Nothing. Pick. We're up." He looked up at the lady behind the counter. "I'll have a scoop of the honey almond and cream in a waffle cone."

"And I'll have a scoop of cookies squared in a waffle cone. Thanks." She smiled at the employee.

"Waffle cone. Good taste," Spencer said with a smirk.

"Are you allowed to eat ice cream without a waffle cone?"

"Only if you eat it directly out of the pint container."

"You might have an ice cream problem." Clare pulled out her wallet from her pocket, but Spencer paid before she could. After taking her cone, she followed him to a seat outside.

"Thanks for the ice cream." She lifted her cone as if to toast the occasion.

He lifted his as well, but didn't take a bite right away.

"Are you watching me?" Her mouth hovered over the ice cream.

"I want to see your reaction." His brown eyes didn't stray from hers.

"Okay, weirdo." She licked the treat, then took a big bite. The sweet, delicious dessert melted in her mouth. She moaned and mumbled, "Oh, this tastes so good."

His smile almost blinded her. "Yep. You'll never want anything else." He took a bite of his, crunching on an almond.

"You know, Maggie doesn't bite into ice cream." He licked the side of the cone, making her a bit jealous of his cone.

She looked down at her own ice cream, now melting down her hand. "Yeah."

"Yep. Says she doesn't like the cold on her teeth. She just licks the whole thing."

"Sounds inefficient."

"It is. And she hates watching people bite the ice cream or a popsicle." The grin on his face looked like one her cousin had any time he teased his sister.

"She's like family, huh?"

"Yeah. Like a cousin or a sister. I don't remember a time when I didn't know her. She and Emma have been best friends forever."

"And you bite into all cold desserts with great enthusiasm when she's near?"

"Yep. Just need to get in her line of sight."

She laughed. "That's so mean."

They settled into a comfortable silence, watching the crowds while they ate. She hadn't taken an opportunity to visit the downtown area much since she moved. The crowds walked down the street, pointing at stores in the distance. Kids pulled on their parents' hands, trying to convince them to get ice cream. She watched the sun sink in the sky, highlighting church steeples over the buildings. Her eyes caught his. He didn't even pretend to not look at her. She fidgeted with the napkin, the only thing left from her snack.

"What?" she asked.

"You have some ice cream on her cheek."

"Oh." She took her napkin and wiped off her mouth. "Did I get it?"

"No." He leaned over close enough that she could feel his breath. He took his own napkin and whipped her face clean. "I got it," he whispered.

She couldn't breathe with him so close, her heart thumped in her chest. It would only take an inch or two to close the distance between their mouths, but she couldn't move. Their eyes steadily stared into each other's.

Then his lips met hers. A quick, chaste kiss. Enough to make her eyes widen. He leaned back in his chair, looking out into the street. "Next time, we'll go to one of the candy shops so you can compare." He looked at her like nothing had happened two seconds before. "You ready to head back?"

All she could do was nod and follow him to his car.

Chapter 9

Spencer

Monday felt like a blur to Spencer. He worked a blood drive downtown, then made it to practice right on time. Clare greeted him with a warm smile. He'd worried that the kiss he gave her was a mistake. She seemed in a daze when he dropped her off.

Clare looked relaxed and didn't avoid his eyes. He could feel his wolf nudge him. The pressure from the fur ball made it hard to concentrate and stay put. No one liked a crowded mic.

Keon caught his attention, raised eyebrows, and a shrug, asking the question without words. Spencer shook his head. No, he hadn't told her. Keon rolled his eyes, then rolled his eyes at Tick. Tick mouthed 'of course' at Keon. He sat back on his drum throne with a huff and a shake of his head.

"At what point am I going to know how to have a conversation with the rest of you without words?" Clare looked between the three of them.

"I give it a month," Tick said.

Keon rolled his eyes. "More like six."

Tick laughed and strummed their bass. "Have faith, Keon. You're a drummer. You know that timing is everything."

He pointed a stick at them. "I hate you."

"You love me." Tick stuck out their tongue.

"I'm ready if you all have finished your silent communication." Clare laughed at Keon's pouty face.

"Fine. Let's hit it." Keon clacked his sticks together and they played the first song on the playlist.

The more they practiced, the more Spencer's shoulders relaxed. He didn't believe they could put together a gig in less than a week. He had to hand it to Keon. He found the right person to pull it off. It saved the group from canceling the gig, which they hated to do, and introduced Spencer to the love of his life.

Before he knew it, practice ended. Spencer wanted to take Clare to dinner. The more time they spent together, the more comfortable she would be when he told her the truth. Right?

He rushed to put away his equipment, which wasn't necessary, as Clare and Tick talked while they packed. Their quiet conversation floated to him.

"Everyone started to call me Tick in grade school. When I'm nervous, I have a very noticeable eye twitch. It's not as noticeable now. I have a little control over it, but it's still there when anxiety hits me."

"What's your real name?" Clare leaned on the mic stand.

"Josie." Tick frowned.

"Josie? As in the pussy cat?"

"And that's one reason why I prefer Tick."

Clare laughed. "I can understand that."

Tick leaned closer to her. "So, what did you do with Spencer yesterday? You give him a chance?"

"Nosey. He took me for ice cream downtown. It was nice."

"Still worried, though?"

"Yes. No. I don't know. I just don't want to be kicked from the band at this point. So, what about you? You have anyone?"

"Don't turn this around on me."

"You want in my business, then I'm in your business."

Tick's eyes widened. "I'll never ask you anything ever again."

Clare laughed, with Tick joining quickly after. Clare's face lit up with joy, wrapped around his heart. He wanted to make her laugh, wanted to laugh with her. At what point would she share that face with him while in his arms, tucked away, warm and safe? Together.

"You're drooling," Keon whispered. "Whatever you're going to do, do it now. I have other shit to do."

"Like what?"

"Sleep."

Spencer nodded and walked up to the two laughing. Tick winked at him and turned away, hauling their gear to their car. Clare turned to him with a smile.

"So, I was wondering…" Spencer began. His phone rang. With a frown, he looked at the caller. Maggie. "Hold that thought." With the phone to his ear, he turned away. "Hey. Whatcha need?"

"That's what I get? Whatcha need?"

"I also said 'hey.'"

"Worst brother ever."

"I'm not your..."

"Anyway," Maggie interrupted. "I need you to make a delivery tonight."

"Tonight?" His voice cracked, but he didn't care. The last thing he wanted to do was drive who knew how long to make a delivery. Didn't Maggie realize he wanted to spend time with Clare?

"Yes. And I'm sorry. It's only to Columbia, South Carolina."

"You're killing me. That's still two and a half hours one way."

"I know. Can you do it?"

"Yeah." He sighed and rubbed his forehead. "Where are you?"

"The shop. Thank you, Spencer. I'll pay you in doggie biscuits."

He growled. "Do you want me to change my mind?"

"Nope. See you in a few."

He ended the call and turned to Clare. "Anyway, I was going to ask you to have dinner with me, but I can't now. I have a job."

He looked away, but could feel her eyes on him. "Want me to help you take your stuff to your car?"

"Yeah. That would be nice." He picked up his amp and his bag filled with cables and pedals.

She followed behind with his guitar. He loaded the car, then turned to her. She stood with her hands in her pockets. She wore what he assumed were work clothes, black slacks and a pale blue button-up blouse. The top few buttons were open and he could see the top of her cleavage. He suddenly wondered if she wore her shirt like that at work.

Swallowing his sudden jealousy, he smiled at her. "Thanks for your help. I'll see you tomorrow?"

"Yeah. I'll be here."

He leaned in and kissed her cheek before climbing into his old Volvo. He watched her in his rearview mirror for a block before he turned the corner.

~

Clare

Clare thought about the kiss on her cheek longer than the one on her mouth. The innocence and purpose of the natural action sent goosebumps over her body. She'd never reacted that way to a kiss on the cheek or even a chaste kiss on the mouth. She wondered, not for the first time that day, how it would feel if he kissed her elsewhere, like her neck or nipples. A shiver covered her body at the thought.

Now she sat in her car outside Keon's house trying to calm her heart before she unloaded for the last practice before the show. She wasn't sure she could play and not stare at Spencer the entire time. Her head rested on the steering wheel. This was so stupid. Of course, she could play without looking at him. She had some self-control. The problem was after practice. And what if Tick was wrong and he was playing with her? Clare didn't know if she could take it again, especially with someone who made her heart skip a beat from a kiss on the cheek.

After exiting her car, she hauled her equipment into the garage and set up with Keon and Tick. Tick talked to her for the next ten minutes while they waited on Spencer. She glanced at her watch every minute, but didn't worry until Keon paced in front of the garage.

"Is that bad?" she asked Tick, pointing at the drummer.

"Yep. He's never this late. And if he is, he usually sends us a message."

Keon eyed the street as he paced. A drumstick twirled between his fingers the entire time.

Clare picked at the strings on her guitar. "Want me to set up my looper? I mean, he knows what he's doing, right?"

Keon checked his watch. "It's been twenty minutes. I'll call."

He pulled out his phone and walked into his yard, pacing the length of the house. Clare noticed Tick's eye begin to twitch. Just enough for her to notice, but only because she knew about it.

"Should we be worried?" she asked.

"Nah." Tick's eye moved again. "He probably got stuck at work or something."

She didn't believe them, but decided against calling them out on it. There was something they didn't want to tell her, and it didn't feel like the time to ask. They'd only met last week, so the group might not trust her.

Only a week. It felt like months. She fit with these people. She fit with Spencer. A groan almost escaped her. What was she doing? He acted just like Brady. Cool and confident. He played the guitar like he picked it up at birth. But Brady never looked at her like Spencer did, like he was holding his breath.

That didn't mean much. He broke her heart, kicked her out of the band, harassed her at work afterward, and became the reason she moved away from her family. A new job, a new city, and a fresh start away from an egotistical bastard. As much as she wanted to give Spencer the chance he deserved, she couldn't bring herself to trust him just yet.

Keon walked back into the garage. "I can't get a hold of him or Emma. I'm sure it's a family thing. Let's practice the best we can. Clare, set up the looper if you don't mind."

He rubbed his face with one of his hands and sat at his drum set. With wide eyes, Tick helped Clare set up the pedal and, within ten minutes, they started practice.

Clare had a rough start with the first song but found her stride in the second. She looped the rhythm and managed to play lead and sing. Her attempts at embellishments and solo parts weren't as clean as Spencer's, but it didn't make the songs worse. After the third song, Keon's phone rang, startling the group.

"Sorry, I turned the ringer up." He answered. "Where are you?"

Clare could hear mumbles on the other side. She waited for Keon to give them an update.

"Again?" Tick said. They seemed to understand the conversation and began to pack up their stuff.

"What's happening?" Clare whispered to them.

"Um..." Tick frowned and looked at Keon, who ended his call.

"We gotta go." He stood and put away his sticks.

"What?" She didn't know what to think.

"Sorry, Clare. We have an emergency. I hate to do this, but we have to go. We'll see you Thursday here to pack up the van." He went inside his house and came out with keys in his hand.

"There's a van?" Clare asked while she put away her equipment.

"Yeah. We'll go over it later." Tick handed her a cable.

After Clare had all her equipment packed up, Tick and Keon grabbed her things and ushered her to her car. As the garage door closed, she turned to watch them rush to the old Toyota in Keon's driveway. They were gone by the time she loaded her car.

The street looked normal. Kids rode bikes down the sidewalks and people walked their dogs. Yet she stood and stared back at the house. The restored Impala was still in the driveway, not rolled into the garage. Dread slowly crept over her. Did something happen to Spencer? But wasn't Keon talking to him? What happened that required all of them to leave in such a hurry?

The thoughts swirled in her mind as she climbed into

her car and drove home.

Chapter 10

Spencer

The old live oaks swayed in the light breeze. Spencer could see just over the tops of most of them from this position on top of Herbs and Healing. He'd spent over an hour combing the streets west of the shop. The person who attacked Maggie was nowhere to be found. He couldn't catch a scent. None of them could. He traveled over ten square blocks before he walked back. Now he sat on the roof, hoping he'd smell something through the breeze, something in the trees.

Maggie escaped with only a scratch on her arm. Mumbles from the bottom floor made their way up to the roof. Ethan and Sylvia argued with her. She wouldn't walk away from this without some kind of guard. The hunters wanted her, and changing her hair color and scent didn't stop them. It only delayed the attack.

Ethan called a meeting ten minutes ago. The pack would gather here. Maggie would get a detail, whether she liked it or not. An old Toyota parked a block away, and he watched Keon and Tick climb out. He jumped onto the oak to his right and climbed his way down. He hung from the lowest branch and fell to his feet in front of his bandmates.

"Does Maggie know you were on the roof?" Keon asked.

He shrugged. "Come on. Let's get inside."

The bells on the door clanged as they entered. Most of the pack was already in attendance, crowding the shop. He looked through the crowd, recognizing many coven members as well.

Ethan looked over at him with his eyebrows raised. He shook his head. No, he didn't find anyone. Ethan frowned and turned back to Maggie and Sylvia. Emma stood behind Maggie with her arms crossed. Someone already treated Maggie's cut. He could see a white bandage peeking out from under her shirt sleeve.

A rumble reverberated through the room. All the wolves quieted down. Sylvia held up her hand, snapping her fingers, and a hush fell over the room.

"The hunters are after Maggie. Today she was attacked for the second time in a week. Sylvia and I ask people to volunteer to stay by Maggie's side in shifts over the next few weeks. They will be eight-to-ten-hour shifts." Ethan's voice carried well in the small room.

Maggie rolled her eyes, her lips pursed tight. She refused to look at Ethan or Sylvia.

"Spencer, should she be attacked at home, can she be relocated to your house?"

Spencer lived in his family home, while Emma lived

in town. It had five bedrooms and was often used to house transient werewolves. The shifting enclosure for the pack sat on the land, a few minutes' walk behind the house. He thought of Maggie as part of the family. She and his sister had been best friends since before he was born.

"Of course," he said.

"What about Clare?" Maggie stared at Ethan.

"Who's Clare?" He looked back and forth between Maggie and Sylvia.

"My roommate."

Ethan looked over at Spencer.

"She's welcome, too." A spark of excitement lit inside him. His mate might stay at his house.

"Does she know about us?" Ethan looked at Maggie.

"No, but she will," Spencer said.

Ethan raised an eyebrow, but didn't comment. "Okay. Emma's taking the first shift tonight. Come see me to sign up, then talk to Sylvia for any additional instructions and equipment."

"This is ridiculous!" Maggie shook her head and pushed her way into her workshop, Emma hot on her heels.

"You going to sign up?" Keon asked.

"Yeah. That's what I do, right?" Spencer crossed his arms. "I'll wait until the line dies down."

"Do you think you'll have the time?"

He sighed. "I'll find it."

"You're going to burn out, my man." Tick grabbed his shoulder.

"He's going to sign up for all the night shifts so he can sneak into Clare's room." Keon waggled his eyebrows at Tick, whose laugh drew the attention of those around them.

"I hate you both."

Keon swung his arm around his shoulder. "You love us. And you'll be the happiest wolf in town once you spill the beans to your lady."

"He's gotta get the guts first." Tick poked him in the stomach.

"You know, for someone who acts on instinct, makes rash decisions in the heat of the moment, you sure are dragging your feet," Keon said.

"She makes me so nervous. What if I do it wrong? What if she walks away? Forever?" He stared out across the store, a frown stuck to his face.

"I didn't know you could be nervous." Tick hugged him around the middle, then walked over to the dwindling line.

"Let's go sign up, lover boy."

Spencer followed the two of them.

He stood around, waiting for a chance to do his part. Since his father died, Emma really stepped up as an asset to the pack. He followed in her steps when he graduated high school. While Ethan might be in charge, he leaned heavily on the Luvels. They let him. It filled a hole left by the death of their father.

But Spencer felt stretched thin over the last few weeks. Work, music, and pack duties didn't give him the time he needed, the time he wanted, to spend with Clare.

And Emma's stunt on Saturday weighed on his mind. He watched her huddle with her best friend. Maggie and Emma always worked together when the pack and coven came together. His two sisters. And Maggie needed to lean on others now. He knew she hated it. And Emma couldn't be there all the time. Emma needed to rest, too.

He walked past the sign-up sheet and pulled Emma away from the crowd. Maggie raised an eyebrow, but didn't follow.

"What are you doing?" Emma jerked her arm out of his hand.

"Are you sure you'll be able to protect her tonight?"

"Yes. Of course."

"Let me check your pulse." He reached up to touch her neck.

"Stop." She knocked his hand away. Her eyes turned golden. The wolf inside her that couldn't escape even under the full moon stared at him.

"Stop?" He grabbed her hand, unphased by her eyes. "You were dangerously low on iron four days ago. I don't want you to collapse."

Her eyes faded to brown, and she relaxed by his side. Her wrist flipped over for him to feel her pulse. The blood pulsed under his fingers, stronger than Saturday. His body let go of the tension it'd held since she almost passed out.

"You're good. Better than Saturday, actually. Thank you for taking care of yourself."

She leaned in, her forehead resting on his. "Thank you for being a good brother."

She ruffled his hair and walked back over to Maggie,

who gave him a wink. She must have gotten on Emma's case as well.

By the time he reached the sign-up sheet, there wasn't an open spot.

A hand clasped on his shoulder. "You'll be our backup. And you're needed to make deliveries." Ethan smiled. "Now, tell me how you know Maggie's roommate."

~

Clare

The house was dark when Clare parked her car. Not an unusual sight, but it still made her uneasy after the way the group acted when she left.

"Is Maggie still treating you well?" her ammachi asked over the phone.

"Yeah. She's still great. Though she dyed her hair brown recently. She looks more normal with blue hair."

Her ammachi laughed. "Her personality is colorful. Tell her I said to dye it back. Now tell me more about the boy."

"How did you learn about him again?"

"I have my ways. Does he like music?"

"Yeah. I joined his band." She made her way to the back door and flicked on the kitchen light. She put down her guitar and leaned on the kitchen island.

"Oh. He's not like the last boy, is he?" Her voice darkened, sending shivers down Clare's spine.

"I don't think so. He doesn't work with me, which is

a plus. He's similar to Brady, but not at the same time. More attentive, in a way. Softer. His priorities center around his family."

"He has a family that he likes. That's a good sign. What's his name?"

"Spencer. Spencer Luvel, I think."

"Luvel? Does that mean wolf in French? Or is that Lowell?"

"I don't know. You research that kind of thing, not me."

"Is he Maggie's friend's brother? Emma?"

"Yeah. He is. You and Maggie must talk a lot."

"She's a great friend. A good listener. She keeps the magic alive, you know."

"You've always said stuff like that about magic and the secrets of the world. Do you really believe it?"

"Yes. And I also believe your wolf boy is much different from the one before. Loyal. I can hear it in the name. Luvel."

Clare laughed. "Okay. I'll let you know if you're right."

"Have I ever been wrong?" Her grandmother's voice hitched up a notch.

"Yes. That cat you had was part bobcat and not a short-tailed Maine Coon."

"Once. I was wrong once. Trust your ammachi. I need to go. Love you, child."

"I love you, too."

After the call, she brought in the rest of her equipment and left it near the base of the stairs. She'd bring it up after she ate. Clare pulled out some thawed chicken and heated up a pan. The rice she made yesterday still sat in the fridge. It would go well with the chicken. Clare grabbed a jar of hot honey and added it to the chicken, then a dash of soy sauce and a few minced garlic cloves.

She cooked it all together, then laid it out on the cold rice. Would Spencer like this? All her family ate spicy food, and Keon mentioned Spencer wasn't the biggest fan. Why did she want him to like her cooking?

She stood at the island and ate her food when the backdoor opened. Maggie walked in, followed by Emma, who dropped a large bag on the floor.

"Welcome home," Clare said with a mouthful of chicken.

Maggie sighed. "Hey. Emma's gonna stay the night on the couch."

"Don't you have another guest room?" She looked at the two women. Maggie's lips were tight.

Emma shook her head. "The couch is fine with me. I can hear more there."

"What's going on?" She studied Maggie as she leaned on the counter. A white bandage peaked out beneath her shirt sleeve. "What happened to your arm?"

Maggie glanced over her shoulder at Emma. Emma nodded back at her. Maggie rested her head on the counter. "I was attacked at the shop today."

Clare barely heard her through the muffled voice. "Attacked? That's terrible. What's being done?"

Emma rested a hand on Clare's shoulder. "The cops

know, and since we can't get a police presence, several of her friends will be with her over the next few days. So, expect a few house guests."

Clare stared at Emma. She had the same brown eyes as Spencer, only lighter. This close, she could see their resemblance. "Why would you guard her after one attack? Was it not just a robbery?"

The look Maggie and Emma gave each other worried Clare.

"Is that why you colored your hair? Were you attacked before?" Her voice pitched higher and higher the more she spoke.

"It's fine. I'm fine. Don't worry. I don't need you to freak out, too." Maggie pushed off the counter and walked off. "I'm going to bed."

"What about my sheets?" Emma put her hands on her hips.

Maggie waved her hand in the air. "You know where they are."

They watched Maggie as she left and listened to her footsteps travel up the stairs.

"Is there anything I can do?" Clare asked.

With a sigh, Emma shook her head. "Not right now. Not tonight. Just keep the doors and windows locked. Pay attention to your surroundings. Call me if you see anything weird."

"How weird are we talking?"

"The lowest level of weird."

Chapter 11

Clare

Emma still slept on the couch when Clare left in the morning. She checked her rearview mirror every five seconds on the drive to work. Maggie was the one in danger, yet Clare's paranoia didn't lessen the further she got from the house.

Her thoughts remained on the situation while she tried to focus on her job. They weren't telling her everything. The situation didn't make sense. Why would anyone want to attack Maggie? Did she cheat someone on an order? Did someone actually expect her spells to work? Clare shook her head at the ridiculous nature of people. They'd believe anything. Maggie's life shouldn't hang in the balance of someone else's bad decisions.

Someone else would be with Maggie tonight. The likelihood of her knowing them was slim. She'd only met about five of Maggie's friends and family. Her thoughts turned to Spencer. He could be there, sleeping on the couch, just one floor away from her, steps from her own bed.

Did he sleep with his shirt off? Would he risk the chance to sneak into her room? She shook her head out of those thoughts, ignoring how her chest tightened at the idea. The computer screen she stared at waited for her. This document needed to be finished before she left, but her thoughts were consumed by Maggie and now a mostly naked Spencer. What if he slept completely nude?

She jumped from her seat and took a walk around the building. The rest of the day wouldn't get any better.

When she arrived home, she found a man with shoulder length black hair studying in the dining room. Maggie lay on the living room floor with her legs on the couch, staring at the ceiling fan.

"Want me to cook dinner tonight?" Clare asked.

Maggie's dark hair fanned around her head like a halo, highlighting her pale skin.

"Sure." Maggie didn't even look her way. "This is Pablo. He's staying the night. Pablo, this is Clare, the roommate."

Clare waved at Pablo as he looked up from his book and nodded at her.

"He's dating Hayley, Chucker's sister."

"Chuck. He's with Jesi, right?" Clare sat on the couch next to a pair of feet.

"Yep."

"I can make you butter chicken, tacos, or I can order us Chinese."

"Ooh, make enchiladas," Pablo interjected.

"She's Indian, not Latina." Maggie threw a tuft of

carpet Pablo's way.

"Yeah. Doesn't mean she can't make enchiladas."

"I've given three choices. Maggie chooses one, or you both are on your own. And I've never made enchiladas."

"I'll give you a recipe, and you can make Indian enchiladas." Pablo stared off into space with his head resting on his hand.

Clare looked at Maggie with a frown. "Someone has a craving."

"Sounds like a him problem." Maggie smiled up at Clare. She shot her hand up toward her. Clare grabbed it and pulled her into a sitting position.

"Chinese sounds good. I'll go grab a menu. Tomorrow won't be so bad. I can go to your show."

"Will that be safe?" Pablo stood and followed them into the kitchen.

"Yeah. Plenty of people will be there. I'll have lots of bodyguards."

"You'll have lots of chances to ditch us." Pablo narrowed his eyes at Maggie.

"I won't ditch anyone. I have some sense."

He rolled his eyes. "So, Clare. Keon says the show's going to be great."

"Yeah?" She enjoyed knowing Keon actually believed it.

"Yeah. Apparently, it's all he can talk about at work."

"Do you work with him?"

"Nah. Hayley does."

Clare nodded. She would need to keep all these

people straight if they were associated with the band. She didn't realize how many people that would be. As long as they didn't give her a quiz, she'd be fine.

"Okay, let's order. I'm starving." Maggie gave her the menu.

~

Spencer

Spencer tapped his fingers to the beat of the music as he drove to Keon's house. For gigs, Keon borrowed a van from his boss. They'd load everything up and ride together.

He tried to focus on the upcoming concert, but his mind wandered to Maggie's arm. He didn't know who would be with her tonight, but he liked the idea of Clare being in harm's way even less.

Maggie could take care of herself. He'd seen her fight. Clare probably didn't have any training. She didn't have a clue about the supernatural and was potentially a sitting duck. He needed to talk to her soon. He let out a breath. Tomorrow. He'd tell her tomorrow. They just needed to get through the show.

He parked his car and dragged his equipment over to the van in Keon's garage. Tick popped a bubble at him and smacked their gum at him.

"Really?" He raised an eyebrow and slid his guitar into the van.

"I'm excited. All my stuff is already loaded. We're just waiting for you and Clare."

"Yeah. Where's Clare?"

"On her way. Traffic coming from the airport isn't always the best." Tick danced where they stood. He thought their jeans might drop off their narrow hips, but the belt held strong. They wore a baggy pair of jeans kept up by the belt and a black shirt with the bottom diagonal half a red plaid print.

"Nice shirt." He loaded the rest of his gear.

"Yeah? I made it. Matches my hair."

"It is red today." He reached up and touched the hair that fell into their eyes. They kept the sides shaved and the longer top brushed back, though parts always fell in their eyes. "I like it. Feels better than last time, too."

"I paid a professional. My mom kept telling me it looked fried. I'll go get Keon." They waved at someone behind him and walked toward the house.

Spencer turned to see Clare walk up. She still wore her work clothes, though she carried a duffle bag along with her other equipment.

"Hey. Glad to see you. I didn't know if we could play without you." She dropped the duffle bag and smiled.

"Is that the only reason you're glad to see me?"

She looked down before looking him in the eyes. "No. You're good at carrying stuff, too. Come help me with the rest." She winked and turned to her car.

He breathed her in and followed. He'd follow her anywhere.

~

Spencer

It felt natural to unload the van and set up the stage at the venue. A sense of calm washed over Spencer. After the last week, this was precisely what he needed. To play and to have fun.

He watched Clare fall into the rhythm of the setup like she'd always been there. He rolled the cables to the outlets off-stage, while the rest set up the stage area.

"Hey, Spencer." A high-pitched voice shot through him. He stood and turned.

Jen. The woman he'd maintained a casual relationship with when she didn't have someone steady.

"Hey, Jen. You come here with Ryan?" He surprised himself by remembering the latest man's name.

"No. I dumped him last week." She stepped up to him and walked her fingers up his arm. "I was hoping we could do something after the show tonight."

He brushed her hand off his arm and turned around. "Nah. I'm not interested."

Chapter 12

Clare

Clare looked around the stage. One cable short, and no idea where she put it. She walked towards backstage when she saw a blond woman lightly touching Spencer.

She stopped breathing, in case they could hear her, and hid behind a curtain. She knew eavesdropping wasn't attractive, but she couldn't help herself.

"What do you mean you're not interested?" the woman said in a tiny voice.

"I'm not interested. I don't want to do anything with you after the show."

"Are you kidding? You've never turned me down."

"I'm turning you down now."

"But I love you."

Spencer's laugh sent shivers down her arms. "No, you don't. I'm your backup. Always have been. And I don't want to be that anymore. I want to be someone's first choice, not a placeholder."

"I can't believe you'd say that to me."

The sound of Spencer moving wires filled the silence. Clare almost thought the woman had left until she heard her sigh.

"Who is she?"

"Just someone. I like her. And I don't want to mess it up."

"Is it the new singer? I saw her out there. She's cute."

"What if it is?" He sounded bored.

"Maybe I'll congratulate her."

"Don't go near her. You forget how well I know you. Besides, you're too old for the mean girl act." His dark tone shocked Clare.

"It's not an act. I just can't help myself." Her whine hit an octave that hurt Clare's ears.

"Well, go find your way back to the front and find someone else. You won't be lonely for long."

"Are you going to tell her your secrets?"

"Secrets?"

"Yeah. The ones you wouldn't tell me. Why you really disappear during the week? What really happens when you go off with your sister? The phone calls you told me to not to worry about? Are you going to tell her?"

Clare's heart jumped to her throat as she held her breath.

"Yeah. I'm going to tell her."

Clare swallowed her gasp.

"Lucky girl," she huffed. "I'll see you around, Spencer."

Clare listened to her heels click off the stage area. She waited a minute before she made her way toward him in search of the cable, but first, she needed her heart to slow down.

"Eavesdropping, are we?"

Clare turned to see Spencer staring down at her with a smile.

"I was looking for a cable and didn't want to interrupt." The excuse sounded weak to her own ears.

He laughed and pulled her behind the curtain. He picked up a cable from his pile. "I think this is what you're looking for."

"Yeah. Thanks." She felt her cheeks burn, so she avoided his eyes and turned to leave.

His warm hand wrapped around her upper arm, pulling her back around. With his free hand, he lifted her chin, forcing her to look into his eyes. Even in the dimly lit area, they seemed to glisten.

"I meant it," he said, leaning his face closer to hers. "I don't want to mess this up."

She felt him pull away, but she didn't want to leave yet. Clare reached around his neck and pulled him down to meet her lips. His arms snaked around her body in an instant and deepened the kiss. Spencer's tongue danced with hers as a tingle of need traveled from her lips straight to her core. She wanted nothing more than to wrap her legs around him and mark him with her nails.

"This is nice and all, but we have a show." Keon's voice startled them apart. "Y'all need to tune your shit. I'll finish plugging everything in." He shook his head and pushed them out of the way.

Clare swore she heard him mumble, "stupid mates,"

as they walked away. She wondered what that meant.

~

Spencer

Her voice floated through the crowd. It took everything Spencer had to play and not just watch her and drool. Her black hair shined in the spotlight. The crowd danced to their sound, and whenever he looked back, he saw Keon grinning like an idiot while he played. Tick looked relaxed as well. This would work. Clare was officially the new member.

Despite his desire to stare at Clare the whole night, he scanned the faces in the crowd. No one expected an attack on Maggie, but that didn't mean they should relax. Maggie stood in the middle of members from the pack and coven. She moved to the beat, but her face didn't exactly appear cheerful. More of a grimace from being surrounded.

The place looked busy for a Thursday night, but it might just be the curiosity of those wanting to see the new band member. They weren't the most popular group in Savannah, but they did have a bit of a following.

The energy built around the band. He could feel them playing in sync more than they ever had in practice. The entire situation blew his mind. A week ago, they were contemplating canceling this performance. Now he couldn't wait to have more.

The song ended. One more, and they would be done, besides the encore song. He knew they'd play it. His face felt tight from all the smiling.

"Least of My Kind," someone yelled from the crowd. The request echoed over a few more people. Clare looked back at them, eyebrows raised.

"I can sing it, but I don't know if I can play it."

Tick's eyes grew wide, looking at him and Keon. Spencer shook his head no at the drummer.

Keon's once smiling face soured. "No. We can't play it tonight."

"Last song, then." Clare smiled and pointed at Keon. "Let's go."

When they started the last song, he heard a few sounds of disappointment, but they ended the gig with the anticipated encore.

"Thank you. Thank you. Come back and see us, Wolves on Fire. Goodnight." Clare closed them out, and they left the stage.

All they needed to do was pack up the van and come back for drinks, but all Spencer wanted to do was wrap his arms back around Clare and kiss her senseless.

As they worked to clean up the stage, he pulled Clare behind the curtain again. "Help me unplug all this?"

His lips kissed down her neck, and he held her tight to his chest. Her hands pushed him back.

"Don't give me those sad eyes. We need to get all this back in the van." Her hand touched his face. "Then we can talk about not messing this up."

Her lips touched his for less than a second, and then she walked away to continue packing up. A hand patted him on the shoulder.

"Aww. A werewolf in love." Maggie smiled at him.

"I don't think that helps."

"You wanted my help?" She laughed, took a bag from Tick, and headed out to the van.

"Should she be helping?" he said to no one.

"No, but she managed to get away from her detail." Keon laughed and walked back to the stage.

A yell came from the alley outside.

"Maggie!" Emma jumped onto the stage and raced past the others, now right on her heals.

They pushed past the door leading outside to find Maggie throwing something at a large man, who turned into a hawk and flew off before Maggie's potion splashed on the ground.

"Clare?" Maggie said, looking around.

Clare lay sprawled against a wall, her head bleeding. Spencer rushed to her side.

~

Clare

Clare walked behind Maggie, who held a few bags destined for the van. She remembered seeing her surrounded by a group of people in the crowd during the show.

"Lost your posse?" Clare asked from behind.

Maggie turned and grinned. "For a little bit."

Outside in the alley, Clare climbed into the van and started organizing the equipment so everything would fit. Maggie placed the bags and turned to leave.

"I knew I'd find you alone, eventually." A scruffy voice said.

Maggie's body flew out of Clare's view from inside the van. A large man who must have never skipped arm day stalked by. He wore a bowler hat like he was Mr. Hyde and his eyes looked like beads of black under his wild brown eyebrows.

"Come quietly. You're worth more alive."

"And who exactly wants me?" Maggie said.

Clare's heart pounded in her chest, aware the man didn't know she was there. Without another thought, she jumped onto the back of the man, made easy by jumping from the back of the open van.

"Run Maggie," she yelled, her arm around his anime sized neck, pulling his hair, and knocking off his ridiculous hat.

Clare couldn't see if Maggie ran. The man spun her back and forth, his meat hands tugging at her arm. Once her arms gave out, she sailed into a wall. Her head felt fuzzy and pounded in time with her heart. She tried to yell out to Maggie. Everything spun around her when she tried to look around. It looked like Maggie stood in the middle of the alley, squared off against the scowling, muscled attacker. She couldn't keep her eyes open. They blinked open and closed. Before she couldn't keep them open any longer, the man changed into a bird. She must have hit her head really hard.

Chapter 13

Spencer

Spencer stared down at Clare's awkwardly bent body against the wall. Blood trickled down her face and onto his hands as he checked her neck for a pulse.

Emma slid beside him. "How is she?"

"Her heart's strong. Should we call an ambulance?"

"I'll get my bag," Maggie said behind them, her footsteps faded off in the distance.

"Let's wait until Maggie gets back." Emma lifted one of Clare's eyelids and shined her phone light in them.

"She'll think it's strange we didn't send her to the hospital." He picked up her hand and squeezed it.

"Then I guess we just have to tell her the truth." She glared at him, then turned back to Clare.

"Worst sister ever."

"I love you, too."

"Here, let me sprinkle this over her, then we can move her and have her drink a stronger healing potion." Maggie squeezed in between Spencer and Emma.

After dumping a small bag of herbs into her hand, Maggie sprinkled the contents over Clare.

"Water, Air, Fire, Earth

with strength and health

balance, stabilize, calm

keep her together, whole self as one bound."

The blood stopped flowing down Clare's face, and her breathing deepened. Emma rechecked her eyes.

"Can we move her?" Spencer asked.

"Yes, let's move her inside."

His arms scooped her up in one effortless movement, hugging her safely against his chest as he carried her into the club. He placed her on a table in what the club considered a greenroom, which doubled as storage.

"Here." Maggie placed a small bottle in his hand. "Try to get her to drink this."

He trembled as he lifted her head and poured the liquid into her mouth. She swallowed with a light brush along her throat. He could do nothing besides watch her. Her head lay lifeless in his arms as he waited for her to wake up. Drops of his tears hit her cheeks.

A soft hand on his shoulder took his attention away. "Why don't you lay her head down? I think you need a moment to wash your face."

Emma's voice brought him out of his tunnel vision around Clare. Muffled sounds of the club came through the walls. His lips kissed Clare's warm forehead, and he walked out of the room.

The cool water on his face didn't stop the slow shedding of tears. Blood still stained the bottom of his shirt, though he'd washed it off his hands. A pale figure looked back at him in the mirror. He almost lost her. And yet, she acted so brave, struck against a foe she knew nothing about. He couldn't put off telling her. He'd tell her tomorrow, after she'd rested. God, he was an idiot.

He came over and took her hand in his. Her soft hand squeezed his after a few minutes. His heart sped up, and he leaned over her.

"Clare?"

Her eyes slowly blinked, not quite opening.

"Clare. How do you feel?"

"Spencer?" Her eyes opened, and she placed a hand on his cheek. "What's wrong? Why are you crying?"

"You were thrown into a wall."

"My head hurts. Where am I?"

"We're still in the club. Backstage."

"But why are you crying?"

He rubbed his face. "I was worried about you."

"About me? What happened?"

"Someone attacked Maggie, and you jumped in. You hit your head when he pushed you down."

"Don't worry, you're fine." Emma patted her arm. "Humans aren't much different than animals."

~

Clare

Clare rubbed her head as she pushed herself into a sitting position. "I must have imagined that guy turning into a bird."

Spencer wrapped his arm around her back, warming her instantly. "Come on. I'll take you home."

"What about my car? What about Maggie?"

"I'm here. No worries." Maggie waved from across the room. "We will have extra people at the house tonight. Keon said he'd get your car back to you tonight."

"Okay." She leaned against Spencer. Once she stood up, her legs wobbled a little.

Spencer walked her out to his car. She felt small in the passenger seat. The lights flashed past her as he drove, his right hand clutching her left. His touch calmed her, though she still trembled at odd intervals. Would she be able to sleep tonight? She didn't know.

When he pulled into Maggie's driveway, her car was already there. She wondered, *how long was I out*? He helped her into the house and put water on to boil as soon as she sat down at the island.

"Maggie keeps a tea around here that should help you sleep. I'm sure she'll want some, too." He went through the cabinets until he found what he sought, a small jar of loose tea hand-labeled 'Restful Sleep.' He stood with the jar in his hand and a blank look.

"Does she do this as a pot or individual cups?" he muttered.

Maggie walked in before he could decide. She looked over at him after she dropped her bag on the bench near the door. "Make a pot, please."

A man with hair graying on the sides and a man with short curly black hair who resembled Keon walked in after Maggie.

"You must be Clare," the man with the graying hair said.

"Yes." She shook the hand he offered her.

"My name is Ethan, and this is Isaiah. It's nice to meet you." He looked her straight in the eyes. His stare made her want to fidget, but she didn't look away. "Thank you for trying to help her tonight. Don't do it again."

He turned to Isaiah, nodded, then walked back outside.

"Where is he going?" Clare asked before she could stop herself.

"He's going to check the area for anything suspicious. It's nice to meet you. Keon's told me a lot about you and I enjoyed the concert tonight." Isaiah shook her hand with a smile.

"You have to be his dad."

"I know. He gets his good looks from me." He smiled, nodded at Maggie and Spencer, then left the room.

"He's going to check the house." Maggie sat down next to her.

"How are you feeling?" she asked.

"I should ask you that question." Maggie hugged her with one arm, then rested at the island.

Silence settled over the two of them as they watched Spencer pull out a teapot and put some of the loose tea inside. Only the soft sounds of Spencer's movements broke the room's silence. Once the kettle boiled, he poured it over the leaves in the pot and covered it.

"Six minutes?" he asked.

Maggie nodded.

Before she knew it, Spencer placed a cup of tea in front of her. She watched Maggie take a sip before she took her own. The warm liquid slid down her throat and settled in her stomach. A calm overtook her almost instantly. She took another sip.

She finished her tea while she watched Spencer clean up the teapot. This couldn't be the first time he'd washed a teapot. His actions were methodical and purposeful, wiping each surface clean. He treated the delicate pot with care before he placed it in the dish rack to dry. Once the cups were empty, he grabbed both and cleaned them with the same care as the pot.

Her limbs felt heavy when Isaiah and Ethan walked back into the kitchen.

"The inside is clear and secured," Isaiah said.

"Everything is clear outside as well." Ethan put a hand on Maggie's shoulder. "One of us will sleep on the couch. Where would you like the other to sleep?"

Maggie's eyes looked weak when she turned to Ethan. When she spoke, Clare could barely hear her. "I don't know. Wherever you think is best."

Ethan kissed the top of her head. "I'll sleep on the floor of your room. Alright, let's all go to bed. It's been a long day. Spencer, are you staying?"

"No. I'll head out now." He squeezed Clare's hand on the way out. "I'll talk to you tomorrow."

Clare nodded. Watching him leave left an emptiness inside her. He should stay, she thought. She didn't know why that thought appeared. Exhaustion must have come over her. They barely knew each other. Why would he stay for her? What would he think if she asked him?

Chapter 14

Spencer

The afternoon's heat beat down on Spencer outside the Red Cross building. At the moment, it felt better than the freezing temperatures inside. Typically, the cold didn't bother him, but he didn't sleep well. His thoughts drifted back to Clare, and then to Maggie. Would Clare get wounded again? Could they stop the attacks on Maggie before anyone else got hurt?

He should be worried about Maggie, too. The mate pull made it hard for him to focus on anyone but Clare, especially after the night before. Her twisted body on the ground in the alley stuck in his mind. He wasn't there to stop it. Would he always be a moment too late?

He'd already talked to her twice today. He couldn't put off telling her everything any longer. They'd made plans to meet after work. Maybe it wouldn't be a disaster.

~

Clare

Clare looked at her phone for the twentieth time in the past hour. She expected to see a text from Spencer at any moment, at every moment, if she could be honest with herself. She had a rough night and only wanted to wrap herself around him.

What a ridiculous notion. She'd known him for a week. Where did these feelings come from? She rechecked her phone. His last message said he would stop by her house after work, which ended roughly five minutes ago.

Working half days on Fridays gave her extra time to go through her closet. Most of her clothes draped over her bed as if his visit constituted a date. She didn't spend this much time looking for an outfit for a gig. Ultimately, she settled for a pair of black shorts and a plain purple top that almost fell off her shoulders.

Her reflection didn't look too bad, considering her head bashed into a wall the night before. Her budding crush on Spencer might spell doom for the band. She never should have listened to Tick. How could a relationship with Spencer end well? It felt like she couldn't learn from her mistakes. At least she didn't work with Spencer, the only saving grace in the situation. For some reason, she thought it might be worth it.

Her phone dinged, and she almost flung it across the room bringing it to her face.

"I'm leaving work now. The printer exploded toner all over me. I'm going home to shower first. Will you still be there in an hour and a half?"

The message came with a picture of black powder covering half his face and torso. He gave the picture taker a death glare. She enlarged the image to see a co-worker laughing in the background.

She quickly texted back, "Sure. See you then," with a laughing face. Laughter bubbled up as she saved the picture for later.

The extra time increased her anxiety. After five minutes of pacing the floor of her bedroom, she decided to make dinner.

With dinner simmering on the stove, she ran upstairs to brush her hair once more and raced back down.

She answered the front door to find Spencer standing on the porch with damp hair. He wore a plain dark blue button-down shirt untucked over a pair of loose black shorts. One too many of the buttons on the shirt were open.

"Hi." He smiled at her and walked into the house.

"Why did you come to the front door?"

"I don't know. I'm nervous, I guess."

Clare grabbed his hand and guided him into the kitchen. "I made dinner. I hope you haven't eaten."

"I haven't. It smells delicious." He stood in the kitchen, refusing to let go of her hand.

"Do...you want to eat first?"

"Yeah."

"You might want to let go of my hand." She winked

at him.

He dropped her hand with a blush. "Sorry."

"You are nervous." She kissed his cheek and pushed him toward the plates. "My family does things buffet style, so make a plate and sit."

The silence while they ate sat heavily on her shoulders. He avoided looking at her for too long and complimented her cooking too often. She ate slowly, knowing he could feel her gaze on him.

"So...what did you want to talk about?" Her plate sat half empty, but her stomach couldn't hold any more with the building anticipation inside her chest.

"Let me help clean up first." He stood and grabbed both plates. He was in the kitchen before she could speak.

"I can clean up after." She gazed at him from across the room. "I need to know. The dishes can wait."

His brown eyes wavered, but he nodded. "Let's talk outside."

She followed him out the back door. They walked past the greenhouse, and he sat on the bench facing the river. The sun set behind them, darkness slowly surrounding them.

"I don't know how to begin."

"Just begin. Are you nervous?"

"Yes. I don't know what you'll say or how you'll react. I don't want to scare you away." Sad eyes locked onto hers.

"I won't run. Just say it," she whispered.

He took a deep breath. "Remember yesterday when you thought the guy turned into a bird and flew away?"

"Yeah. I must have hit my head pretty hard."

"He did. Turn into a bird and fly away." His eyes didn't turn away, but his frown deepened. "He's a witch. He used a potion to change his form."

"What?"

"There are many dangerous things in this world, many wonderful things in this world, and I'm a part of them. Maggie is a part of them, and the entire band is a part of them. And right now, Maggie is being targeted by the dangerous part."

"...What?"

She jumped when his hand touched hers, but she tried to keep from pulling away. He must be crazy.

"What? Why Maggie?"

"She's a witch. Well, sort of. She's part of a local coven, and there is an organization that is trying to kidnap or kill her. We don't know. She can tell you more, I'm sure."

"And what about you? Are you a witch?"

"You believe me?"

"No. This sounds crazy."

"I'm not a witch," he sighed. "I'm something else."

"Something else?"

"I don't want to scare you away."

A deep growl filled the air. She turned toward the river in time to see an alligator crawl up the bank and slowly shimmer and transform into a man. The skin on his face slowly faded from green scales to tanned skin. The growl turned into a deep chuckle.

His clothes looked surprisingly dry as he sauntered

toward them, stopping a few feet away. A button-down flannel shirt covered his broad shoulders, and he stood a head taller than Spencer. Clare's heart hammered in her chest. What kind of man was this?

"Scare her?" His deep voice sent chills down Clare's spine. "This witch don't scare easy, now do you?"

Spencer stood up, pulling her up with him. "Who are you, and what do you want?"

"I'm not interested in you, son. I'm here for the witch."

"I'm not a witch." Her voice shook.

"You can't fool me. This is the right house. Right hair color. I know you're not full-on magic. You can't be anyone but Maggie Watkins. You're my next paycheck."

"Don't come closer."

"He was an alligator." She whispered.

"I know." Spencer whispered back and squeezed her hand.

"Son, you can just go on. I'm not interested in you." The man shooed him away with the back of his hand, never taking his eyes off her.

"I'm not Maggie." Clare's voice cracked. Spencer pulled his hand out of hers. But she couldn't bring herself to look away from the large alligator man in front of them. Tears poured down her face. Why would he pull away from her?

The man laughed. The deep rumble increased the trembling down her legs.

"This isn't my first time, sweetie. It'll be a whole lot easier if you don't fight back." He held out his hand. His eyes looked from her to his hand and back.

Fear rooted her to the spot, a fear she'd never felt before. None of this could be real. She must have fallen asleep while she waited for Spencer, because this couldn't be happening.

The man took a step toward her, his hand still outstretched. The movement restarted her body, taking her own step backward, almost falling back onto the bench. She heard a low growl a moment before a large brown wolf barreled into the man. He landed on his back with the wolf on top, it's jaws around his neck. He screamed as his arms pushed and swiped at the wolf, only for the animal to dig its back claws into his stomach. Without letting go of the man's neck, it moved its body to the side, clamping harder. The screams from him turned into gurgles. Silence filled the air when the man's limbs stopped moving.

The wolf dropped the man and looked straight at Clare. She took a shuddering breath. What's scarier than a man who turned into an alligator? The thing that took down the alligator man, that's what. She watched the wolf sit beside the dead man and hang its head as if it did something bad. She noticed a white spot on its nose shaped like a heart. It looked blood-stained. Why couldn't she look at anything else?

The wolf grew on the spot. Its fur disappeared, replaced with skin. Its limbs grew longer and leaner. Before she could comprehend it, Spencer stood before her. Naked.

"You're naked." She felt her cheeks burn, but it was

the only thing she could think of at the moment that would keep her from hyperventilating.

"Yeah." He looked down, then back up at her. "Are you okay? We should go inside now."

He took a step toward her. She tried to back up, but landed with her ass on the bench. She didn't know what to do with her arms. They flailed around while she tried to stand. None of this made sense. Spencer turned into a wolf. He killed that man. Was she going to die next?

No. That didn't sound right. Why would Spencer kill her?

Her breathing sped up as she tried to climb onto the bench. What exactly was she running from? The dead man or Spencer?

A warm hand wrapped around hers. "Please. I would never hurt you." He kneeled in front of her, hunched over, making him look smaller. "Take some deep breaths. It will help. I promise."

She looked down at his hand covering hers. His thumb rubbed the back of hers. The movement helped. She took a deep breath and looked up. Those worried brown eyes gazed back at her.

"We should go inside." He stood and pulled her along.

"Where are your clothes?"

"Uh...they don't shift with me, so they're in shreds right now."

"Oh." She looked behind her. Just as he said, strips of his clothes littered the ground. A startled yelp left her when she saw the dead man and she moved faster to be closer to Spencer.

She followed him through the kitchen and into the living room. He sat her on the couch and kneeled in front of her again.

"I'm so sorry that happened. Do you want some water?"

"Why did that guy have clothes on when he changed?"

"What?"

"The alligator guy. He changed, and he had on clothes. But you don't."

"I don't...I don't know. Maybe his clothes were charmed to change with him."

She sat and stared at him, but also through him. Witches. Wolf and alligator people. She didn't know what to think. The soft touch of his hand on her cheek brought her out of her thoughts.

"I know you must be scared and confused. This is not how I wanted to tell you."

"You can turn into a wolf. And you just killed that guy." She felt a tear fall.

"I couldn't let him hurt you. I'd do it again. I hope you don't hate me because of it."

"No. I just...it's a lot, you know?" More tears rolled down her face.

The sound of cars coming up the driveway caught their attention. She wiped her face with the back of her hand. "Who is it?"

"Sounds like Maggie's car. She must be home."

"She can't find you naked in her house." Her heart

sped up again. "You have to change back. A large dog isn't as suspicious as a naked man."

"Clare, she…"

"No, don't argue, just do it."

"I think you're in shock."

"I'm not. I just…just change." The tremors throughout her body felt both violent and calm all at once.

She looked over to see an enormous wolf sitting on the floor next to her. He whined and rested his head on her lap. Clare stroked his large head with shaking hands, scratching when he leaned into her hand. Her shoulders began to relax.

The sound of the front door unlocking startled them both.

Maggie walked into the room with Keon close on her heels. "Why are we coming in through the front door?"

"You need to vary your routine." Keon locked the door behind him. "Don't always leave and enter your house at the same point. Having a set schedule makes it easier for people to hurt you."

"Who told you that?"

"Chuck."

"Good ol' Chuckers."

They both stopped and looked over at Clare and wolf Spencer. Clare gave a forced smile. The only thing she needed to do was not cry.

"I don't have time for that." Maggie gestured toward Clare and walked toward the kitchen.

"I'll ask when I get back," Keon said, following

Maggie.

Clare's head sank forward. She pressed her cheek against the top of Spencer's head. He felt soft and warm on her skin. At that moment, she didn't want to move. Time could stop and she'd be fine. But time kept moving. She'd have to face the truth.

"WHY IS THERE BLOOD IN MY KITCHEN?" Maggie called from the kitchen.

Clare sat up and looked down at the wolf in front of her. His eyes were wide as well and his ears slanted down.

Maggie barged into the living room and stood in front of them. "What happened? Why is there blood and why does it smell like...reptiles?"

"Um...well, there's a thing and..." Clare said, her breathing increased with her heartbeat. She swallowed. What exactly could she say? She wasn't sure what happened, either. "There was..."

Maggie sighed. "Spencer." She looked down at the wolf who wouldn't meet her eyes. "Shift and tell me what happened."

He nudged Clare with his nose, then shifted, standing naked in Maggie's living room.

Chapter 15

Spencer

Standing in front of Clare, naked, while Maggie interrogated him, he'd never felt so exposed. As a werewolf, he was accustomed to walking around nude. Knowing his mate could look at him on display to others made his hands sweat.

"I was trying to explain everything to Clare when an alligator shifter attacked us. He thought she was you. Apparently, they know you dyed your hair dark."

"What happened to the shifter?"

"...He's in the backyard."

Maggie whacked him on the head with her hand. "Are you serious? Did you tie him up?"

"Um...he's dead."

"I honestly don't know if that's worse. Have you called anyone?"

"No, I've been trying to calm down Clare."

Maggie looked down at Clare. Her eyes widened. "Okay. Go grab some clothes from the 'just in case' drawer. You know the rules, no bare butts on my furniture. Keon, let's go outside and take a look. I'll call Aunt Sylvia if you call Ethan while we look."

Spencer grabbed a pair of sweatpants from the drawer. He often teased her about having a drawer full of clothes in random sizes. Nothing ever happened at her house. She always shrugged and said, "Laugh it up. You'll be the first to use it." He shook his head. Damn, she was right.

"Spencer," Maggie whispered. "I think she might be in shock. Stay close and watch her."

He nodded at her while he slipped on the black pants. She looked like she wanted to say something else but only smiled and walked away. He knew what she'd find outside. As long as Clare didn't have to see it again, he could deal with anything Maggie threw his way.

He moved back to the couch where Clare sat. She swayed in her seat, her eyes unblinking. The cushion next to her sank when he sat down. She didn't respond when he put his arm around her shoulder.

"It's okay to relax. Nothing can get you. I'm here, remember?"

Her eyes turned to stare into his. "What about you? What if something gets you?"

"Nothing can get me."

A light kiss on her lips broke the wall holding her up. She sank into his embrace, burrowing her head into his chest. Fingers pulled at his skin as if she tried to hold on for dear life. He ignored the pain and rubbed her back, hoping to add to her sense of safety.

"You can ask me anything you want whenever you're ready." He kissed the top of her head and inhaled her scent.

She never seemed so small before. While he stood at least a foot taller, she always felt larger than life standing next to him on stage and at practice. He pulled her into his lap and hugged her tight. Her warm arms clutched him tighter but slowly stopped trembling. His chest caught her falling tears.

He held her long enough for more people to arrive. He smelled Ethan and Sylvia when they entered the house and heard Emma outside with Maggie and Keon. More would show up.

Clare's grip on him relaxed, and he felt empty when she pushed herself off his lap, hugging her knees to her chest instead. Red, puffy eyes looked up at him. He wanted to hide her away from everyone and everything.

"I think I'm ready to ask questions." Her voice wavered slightly, but her eyes didn't.

"Okay. I'll answer anything."

"You changed into a wolf, right? What are you?"

"Well, I'm technically a werewolf. I was born this way. My dad was a wolf and I'm a wolf."

"But it's not a full moon tonight."

"No. Those of us born as werewolves can change whenever we want. Only those made are limited to shifting only during the full moon."

"Made?"

"Bitten by a werewolf. There's an antidote, but it only works within 48 hours of being bitten."

"That man, was he a weregator?"

"I think so."

"And he wanted to take Maggie?"

"Yeah."

"Is he the reason her friends are following her around and sleeping on the couch?"

"People like him, yes."

"So, there are more?" Her eyes widened.

"Yeah, like the guy at the club yesterday."

She took a deep breath. "He really turned into a bird?"

"He was a witch. He used a potion to change."

They sat for a bit, quiet, while the backdoor opened and closed, people milling about the house. He didn't dare reach for her yet, though his body craved her touch.

"Why wasn't that guy naked when he changed? You said your clothes don't change with you."

He gave her a tiny smile. "He probably had charmed clothes. It's a good idea if you're planning to change from one form to another often. I don't have that need, so I never had a charmed outfit."

"But you don't know for sure?"

"No. But I'm sure Maggie can find out for you if you're really interested."

"No. It just caught my attention, I guess."

Unable to hold himself back, he reached forward and caressed her cheek. She didn't flinch, nor did she lean into his hand.

"Is there anything else I need to know?" Her eyes, still red, looked like they could fill with more tears at any moment.

"Yeah. There is."

"Can it wait until tomorrow?"

"Of course." He leaned forward and kissed her forehead.

A frantic movement from behind the couch caught his attention. Emma waved her hand and motioned for him to follow her.

"I'm going to get you some water, okay?"

She nodded her head. He looked back at her unmoving form before he walked into the kitchen.

"Spencer, can you tell us exactly what happened?" Ethan asked.

He stood by the island along with Sylvia, Keon, Maggie, Emma, Isaiah, Jesi, and Zara. Spencer frowned at the group and told them what happened in the backyard.

"Clever, using the river," Sylvia said. "Our defenses require improvement, don't you think, Ethan?"

"Here we go," Maggie murmured.

Ethan turned to Maggie. "I'm sorry, but we need to move you and Clare away from this house for now."

"This house is the best protected place in the city. The guy didn't even break my shields."

"Still, he managed to slip through," Sylvia countered.

"There is one place that is easy to shield, hard to find, and has enough room for several people to keep watch." Emma looked straight at Spencer when she said it.

"Of course. The house is always open." He tried to keep his excitement of having Clare in his home from bubbling into his tone.

"That's out of the question," Maggie yelled.

Within a minute, the calm discussion dissolved into everyone shouting their best ideas at each other, with Maggie declining them all. The noise echoed in the kitchen, no doubt throughout the entire house.

Spencer's eyes felt big. He'd never seen such a display from these two groups in one place. The unspoken agreement to never argue in front of coven members no longer existed. He imagined the coven had a similar rule of not fighting in front of the pack. The scene in front of him escalated. No one wanted to submit to the other. The stress of looking over their shoulders for the past month and trying to keep Maggie safe culminated in this bizarre moment.

He stood back and watched, knowing Emma's suggestion was the best, but also knowing Maggie hated depending on anyone. But she wasn't the only one at risk. If he hadn't been with her tonight...

He shook his head. That's the last thing he needed to think about. The voices got louder still, hurting his ears. Weren't their ears affected as well?

A movement caught his eye. Clare moved into the kitchen, her eyes wide, her body shaking like she might explode.

"STOP IT!" she yelled. "STOP IIIIIIIIT!" Her voice, loud and shrill, pierced his ears.

He covered them and collapsed on the floor, shaking all over. Once the sound stopped, he looked around. Everyone but Clare lay on the floor, most staring up at her.

"I can't take the fighting," she whispered. She covered her mouth with her hands, confusion written in her eyes.

Spencer pulled himself up and wrapped his arms around her. "I want you to be safe. You can stay at my place. There are extra bedrooms. Okay?"

She nodded into his chest.

"Go pack a bag. We'll leave in ten minutes, okay?"

He watched as she made her way upstairs and turned when she left his sight.

"I think Emma's idea is the best. Y'all can argue about it as much as you want, but I'm bringing Clare with me. She's been through enough."

"But what did she just do?" Maggie asked.

"I don't think she even knows." Emma stuck a finger in her ear and wiggled it around. "Dang, that hurt."

"Pray tell, how do you know her, Maggie?" Sylvia crossed her arms and tilted her head to the side.

"Her grandmother is a customer. We talk to each other on the phone and via email."

"And what do you know about the grandmother?"

Maggie frowned. "Her name is Gayatri. She lives in Philadelphia. She's Indian and knows about magic. Buys some of my teas and spices. We discuss different spells and such. Once, she mentioned she never shared supernatural information with her children or grandchildren."

"Interesting." Sylvia drummed her fingers on the counter. "Create an opportunity for us to speak. She may shed light upon Clare's...ability."

Maggie rolled her eyes. "Sure."

"In the meantime, Maggie, you should stay at Spencer's," Ethan said. "Even if it's just for tonight. Keon, please stay there tonight, too. I'll let the morning shift know where y'all are."

"Very well." Sylvia frowned.

With a heavy sigh, Maggie turned toward the stairs. "Fine."

The tightness in Spencer's heart loosened a bit. Something still bothered him, but he couldn't put his finger on it. Maggie wasn't a hard person to find, but how did they find her at the club? It's not a regular spot. He'd think about it later. Right now, he wanted to get Clare to his home safe and sound.

Chapter 16

Clare

Clare woke in an unfamiliar room. Light shone through the small opening in the gray curtains. A dusky purple colored the walls and her arms wrapped around what felt like a shag body pillow. She squeezed the firm fluff, rubbing her face into it. A grunt from the pillow in question caused her to sit up straight.

Where was she again, and when did pillows make sounds? She looked down at her fingers still laced in the pillow's fur, when she noticed a snout and ears.

Her memories of the night before came back. The alligator man. The ride to Spencer's house. And Spencer checking on her in the night. He'd offered to hold her, but she shook her head. Then he left the room and returned as a wolf, jumped in the bed with her, and laid down. After a moment's hesitation, she curled up beside wolf Spencer and fell asleep with her fingers gripping his fur.

She studied him as he slept. Brown fur covered his entire body, but an adorable white spot in the shape of a heart covered his nose. She wondered if she should be scared, but she felt safe even with him as a wolf.

His soft fur moved under her hand as she petted his head. The desire to kiss the heart marking on his nose became stronger with each minute. Unable to hold herself back, she leaned down and kissed the top of his nose.

His eyes opened and he stared into hers, freezing her on the spot. Now she noticed the golden glow behind his brown eyes. It must happen when he's a wolf. Before she could move, he was human again, inches from her face. The fur under her hand turned to warm skin.

"Good morning," he said.

She could only blink at him. A naked Spencer lay beside her and she was touching his side. If only her heart would slow down.

"How did you sleep?" His hand tucked her hair behind her ear.

"Good." She couldn't bring herself to pull her hand away. "Thank you for staying here last night."

"Anytime."

His smile shone brightly in his eyes, which held the glow. Was the wolf close to the surface? Those eyes drew her in and didn't let her go. All the fear from the last few days disappeared. Sense and rationality flew from her mind, and all she could see was him. She dipped her head down, capturing his lips. Her hand slid to his back, feeling the lean muscles under his warm skin.

His hands sunk into her hair and caressed her face. His touch felt like fire she couldn't dare back away from, so she pulled him closer. She welcomed his tongue with her own, desperately clinging to his kiss and his embrace.

His hands slipped under her shirt and seared her back. He swallowed her moans until he moved his lips down her neck, causing the sounds to echo around the room. She pressed against his body, feeling his hard erection on her leg. Her hands couldn't quite grab that beautiful ass of his, though she tried. She held tight to his back when he palmed her breast, brushing a nipple. A hiss escaped her mouth, and she wrapped her legs around his waist, wanting more.

She rubbed her core on his erect cock, cursing the pants she still wore. His lips met hers once more. She knew her lips would be swollen, but she only pressed harder trying to consume him. Reaching between them, she wrapped her hand around his shaft.

He froze. The glow of his eyes faded. "I'm sorry."

He detangled himself from her slowly, taking care not to cause her physical pain. The sheet piled up on his lap when he sat and rubbed his hands over his face. She reached up and touched his face. He smiled and leaned into the touch, then kissed her palm.

"We can't go any further. There's more I need to tell you. More to me, to us, that's better for you to understand."

"More? How much more?" She wanted to shrink away from him, from the world which opened up to her the night before. What more could there be?

"It's the specifics that you need to know." He kissed her quickly. "Let's get dressed, and I'll make you breakfast."

She smiled. "You can make breakfast?"

"Absolutely."

With a wink, he stood and walked naked out the door into the hall.

~

Clare

She sat at the small kitchen table and watched Spencer flip pancakes and fry bacon. She stared at the sweatpants, which hung low on his hips, almost falling off. His shirt bunched around his waist, exposing his skin. The thought of him standing naked in front of her created an ache between her legs. Crossing them didn't help, but she didn't want the feeling to stop.

He gave her a dazzling smile when he placed a plate of food in front of her. "Dig in."

The first bite made her realize she was starving. He made the pancakes from scratch and they tasted better than all the pancakes she'd ever eaten. They ate in silence other than the yummy noises she made while eating. He smiled each time, and she tried to swallow the sounds, to no avail.

She finished breakfast and took her plate to the sink. "Thanks for breakfast. I'll do the dishes."

Spencer came up behind her. "You don't have to do that. I'll wash the dishes."

"You cooked. I'll clean. Now sit." She pointed the fork in her hand to the table.

"Clean it afterward. There's more I need to tell you."

"I don't think I'm ready for more."

His hands wrapped around hers and led her back to the table. She had a hard time looking at him. What more could he have to say?

"Clare."

She slowly lifted her eyes to his.

"You know that I'm a werewolf. And that there are witches and other were-creatures." He paused and didn't continue until she nodded. "Well, I'm part of a pack. Or really, a group where werewolves can be safe together on the full moons."

"Full moons?"

"Yeah. The night before and after the full moon also cause were-creatures to change."

"Oh."

"We're called The Old Moss Pack. Ethan is the leader, per se. And the witches in the area are a part of a coven called the Moonlight Oak Coven. Ms. Sylvia is in charge there, though I hear Maggie argues with her a lot."

She followed his stare out of the window into the backyard, then looked back at him, rubbing the back of his neck. "I feel like there is more."

"Yeah. Werewolves are also known for having what's called a fated mate, or a soul mate."

Her heart picked up speed in her chest, but she couldn't speak. He wouldn't look at her.

"And we know our mate when we first meet through smell. Even though we know who our mate is, it doesn't mean the person has to agree to it. We still have free will.

It's just harder for werewolves to ignore our soul mate."

"Okay." The word sounded slow and unstable on her lips.

"Um…and you're my fated mate. I've known since you walked into Keon's garage. But I don't want you to feel obligated to be with me." He looked at her through his lashes.

Why were they so long? Her heart pounded at his confession, but all she could think about were his beautifully long eyelashes. And she wanted nothing else but to feel his lips on hers.

"Your eyelashes…" She shook her head. That wasn't important right now. "What does that mean? I mean… How does it change things? What is expected?"

"I guess nothing is expected right now. You won't have to become a werewolf. You can walk away. You can stay. It's your choice. I will never love anyone else, but you can. If you choose to stay and bond with me, we will feel closer to one another. And if we bond and you choose to walk away, I might not…well. It doesn't end well. I'll just say that."

"How many werewolves are mated to non-werewolves?"

"Most of the pack, actually. If you want to talk to any of them, I can arrange it."

"How will we feel closer if we bond?"

"Bonded mates can sense each other's emotions and can feel where the other person is in relation to themselves. How fast that happens after bonding varies from couple to couple. Someone else would need to explain it better."

"So, I would know where you are at all times? And know how you're feeling? So, if I'm mad, you would just know?"

"Basically, but I wouldn't know what you're mad about. We wouldn't be able to read minds."

She watched his face flush red for an instant when she gradually laced her fingers with his. "All of this, that you're telling me, are these the secrets that the girl at the club was talking about?"

"You really were eavesdropping," he chuckled. "Yeah. These are the secrets. The supernatural exists. I'm a werewolf. You're my soul mate. And...I'm already in love with you."

He stared right at her, like he could see into her heart. Her cheeks burned, though she knew he wouldn't be able to tell. She'd known him for less than two weeks and he loved her? She couldn't return those feelings, no matter how much she liked or desired him physically.

"I don't know what to say."

He squeezed her hand. "You don't have to say anything."

He pulled her up from her seat and kissed her hand. "Let's clean up, and I'll show you around the place."

Chapter 17

Spencer

The tour of the house didn't last long. Spencer thought she might be interested in the sound system in the living room, but she loved the study more. The cushioned chairs caught her attention. She pulled a random book from the desk and plopped right down, pretending to read and smoke what he could only guess was a pipe.

"Having fun?"

She hadn't smiled since they left the kitchen, but she grinned from ear to ear. "I feel like a 19th century detective."

"Come on, Sherlock," he said while pulling her to her feet, "let's go traverse the grounds."

"Traverse the grounds. How posh."

She trailed along after him. The fact that she didn't let go of his hand gave him hope. Once outside, he showed her the backyard equipped with a firepit, the unkept garden further out where his father once grew vegetables, and the path to a stream flowing through the property.

"I love this." Clare kneeled and dipped her hand in the water. "It's not too deep, but makes a lovely sound. Is it safe to wade through it?"

"Right now, it is. When we get too much rain, it can become dangerous."

She shook her hands free of water and stood up. "I love this, even if it is boiling hot outside."

"Yeah. It's the hottest time of the year. Come on. I have something else to show you."

He told her stories of his childhood while they walked. She laughed as he told her of the time Emma chased him through the trees, trying to get him to shift to human form so they could go to dinner. And how they had tree climbing competitions, but somehow Emma always won. She enjoyed hearing the stories of his dad holding him by the scruff of his neck when he'd shift in the house, trying to sneak out as a child.

He told her about the lazy days of summer when he helped his dad in the garden, and the time he and Keon followed the stream to where it connected to the Ogeechee River. They were both grounded when they returned after midnight.

"So, Keon is a werewolf, too?" she asked.

"Yeah. Both of his parents are werewolves, so he was born one. Tick is also one, but they were bitten in middle school."

"Ah. Wolves on Fire. I'm guessing the old lead singer was also a werewolf."

"Yeah, but no one in the pack wanted to join after he

left. And you showed up. It was fate. Or at least, fate for me."

She smiled, then looked away from him as they walked. "Wait. What's that?"

"That is where we shift during the full moons."

"It looks like a huge fence. Why is the fence so tall?"

"Werewolves can jump pretty high, and it discourages hunters from getting in. The fence is around 20 feet high. The enclosure encompasses almost a hundred acres. There are several switches inside will electrify the fence should we need it." He smiled at her wide-eyed look. "Do you want to go inside?"

"Can we?"

"Sure." He led her to a door in the fence that blended in so well most people didn't notice it right away and unlocked it.

He locked the door behind them.

"You feel safe in here?" she asked.

"I do. There are plenty of trees, a pond, and a few shelters set up for when it rains. I have many wonderful memories associated with this place. It's part of my home, after all."

"Why is this on your land? You're not in charge, right?"

He started walking her toward the closest shelter. "Well, it's mine and Emma's. She didn't want to live here, though. Our father was the last leader. When my dad died, we couldn't turn the pack away. It's our pack. His father built this place as a sanctuary for wolves, including the house."

"Is that why there are so many bedrooms?"

"Exactly. The enclosure and the property line have expanded over the years. It's a family legacy."

"So, I know about six werewolves?"

"I guess. Me, Keon, Tick, Ethan...who else?"

"Isaiah, Pablo, and Emma."

"Emma's not a werewolf."

"She's not? But she's your sister."

"Yes. But our mom wasn't one. With two wolf parents, you will be a wolf. With one wolf parent, you can be one or the other, human or otherwise. There are more than just werewolves out there. But Emma is special."

"What do you mean, special?"

"You can't tell anyone this. If you do, it could put Emma at risk. I'm trusting you as my mate."

She swallowed and nodded.

"She's what is called a carrier. She cannot shift into a wolf at any time, but can infect others. If she were to bite you, you would become a werewolf. She's also stronger, more agile, and has a greater sense of smell than a regular human. I've seen her take down her fair share of out-of-control wolves."

"What happens if she's bitten?"

"Nothing. But she's important to the pack as a defender and because her blood is the key ingredient in the antidote for a werewolf's bite."

"Saturday."

"Yeah. Hunters across the Southeast have been infecting humans, and the packs are trying to keep that from happening. And one way to do that is to have the antidote on hand. Maggie's been busy. And Emma doesn't want to let people down. She's going to want me to draw her blood today, too. It's dangerous."

"And you're worried."

"Of course. She's my sister. The only family I have left."

Clare wrapped her arms around his middle and pulled him close. Her head rested on his chest. He wondered what she thought of the speed of his heartbeat. In the enclosure, surrounded by the tall, green trees, he embraced his mate and wished for her to accept him.

"Come on. That shelter has a tunnel that leads back to the house. I want to show you."

He pulled away from her but held tight to her hand. The large wooden building had two doors and three windows, with an air conditioning unit installed in two of them. The inside of the building was outfitted with ceiling fans. Folding tables and chairs leaned against the walls. A ramp wrapped around two sides of the room leading down into the tunnel. A staircase also led down into the tunnel. Each time he walked into the building, he remembered the effort it took to add the ramp with his dad cursing when he realized they needed to increase the size of the building to accommodate the run length.

"Wow. This is a big, empty building." Clare peaked over the railing into the tunnel.

"It's useful when it's raining. We have several smaller shelters, but this one holds the path to the house. People can walk through the woods, too. It was built as a safety measure and for protection against the weather."

He walked her down the ramp and into the tunnel. He flipped the switch, lighting up the long hallway leading to the house. The walls and ceiling were made of concrete. He never thought to ask his dad how they managed that feat, though Ethan probably knew.

Tall, vertical cubbies, much like open lockers, lined along the tunnel walls used to hold the pack's clothes and other valuables while they shifted. He paused at several large trunks beside the cubbies and opened one. Inside were towels, blankets, and pillows.

"If it's raining or cold we can pull the stuff out of these trunks to use in the shelter."

Clare leaned down and ran her hand over some of the blankets. "They're so soft."

"Thanks. I didn't buy any of them." He laughed and closed the lid. "The pack members donate things they think we need."

~

Clare

She put her hand through the crook of his arm as they walked through the tunnel in silence. The tunnel ended in a room added behind the garage and beside the kitchen. They walked up a ramp out of the tunnel into an enclosed space built for the ramp. At the top of it stood two doors, one to the right and the other straight ahead.

Spencer pointed to the one on the right. "That's the garage."

Clare followed him through the other door, which led to a small hall into the dining room. She glanced at her watch. Only an hour had passed. It felt closer to half the day.

"Emma will be here in an hour. I wonder if Maggie is up."

"Oh Spencer," Maggie's voice came from the kitchen. "Can I use this food processor?"

With big eyes, Spencer went to the kitchen. Clare stood in the doorway.

"For what?"

"For an amulet." Maggie smiled like a small child at him.

"Are you putting anything in there that is not food?"

"···maybe," she muttered under her breath.

"Then no."

She frowned. "I'll clean it up."

"Will you buy me a new food processor if you break that one? And can you guarantee the processor will have zero residual magic?"

"How about I only use it for food products and add the non-food products after? No residual magic."

"Go ahead."

Clare tried not to laugh as he walked out of the kitchen. "What is she making?"

"I find it's better not to ask."

"Are you worried she'll blow up your kitchen?"

"No. She hasn't destroyed anything at her house or the shop so, it should be fine."

"What's residual magic?"

Spencer smiled at her and jerked his head down the hall, past the front door. She followed him into the living room. He sat on the couch and pulled her down, almost on top of him. Her cheeks felt flushed, but she didn't move.

"Residual magic happens when part of a spell has rubbed off on an object or person. Whenever someone thinks their toaster or oven is haunted, it's usually residual magic. It's rarely harmful, just a pain to deal with."

"What happens when it rubs off on a person?"

"They might act strange for a few days, but it goes away with enough sleep. Sometimes non-magical kids born to magical parents will have residual magic. They can see magical barriers, but can't actually harness the power as their family does."

Clare leaned her head on his shoulder. "There's a lot to learn, isn't there?"

"Yeah. But I hope you have plenty of time to learn it."

He squeezed her hand and kissed it. She soaked up his warmth, but needed more. She turned his head toward her and kissed him. He responded immediately. His hands sunk into her hair, and she grabbed his shirt, pulling him closer. Her back hit the couch with him on top of her. A tightness that started in her heart led straight to her core. Was this what it felt like to be in love? Was this the bond he talked about?

She only knew that she never felt this way before. So, she clung to him and tangled her tongue with his, desperate and wanting.

"Spencer." Someone called his name from the other room.

She looked up at him as he pulled inches away from her face. His mouth looked slightly swollen and his cheeks burned red.

"Ugh. Emma." He rested his forehead on hers. "I'm sorry. I got carried away."

She kissed him. "I like it when you get carried away."

"I only want to get carried away if you decide to stay. I don't want to watch you walk away."

He rolled off her and walked out of the living room.

"Let's set up in the dining room or the kitchen. Either is fine," Spencer said.

"Sounds good. Where's Maggie?"

Clare lay on the couch and stared at the ceiling, touching her lips. Did she plan on staying? Did he mean at his house or stay as his mate? He had to mean as his mate. She couldn't possibly move into his home after such a short period. That's what he meant. She's his fated mate...right?

Chapter 18

Spencer

Spencer finished taking the few vials of blood from his sister he was willing to draw. Having Maggie watch over it this time lifted a weight off his mind.

"You can take more." Emma almost sneered at him.

"No. Your health is also important." He pulled the needle out of her arm and made her apply pressure to the site.

"Don't pout. If you die because he draws too much blood, I'm killing him, too." Maggie said.

"I still think you can take more. Especially if you get Clare to sing to me again."

Spencer felt his eyebrows nearly touch his hairline. "What?"

"Yeah. She called to my wolf. It felt weird, but I had a much better week. It felt like she could almost pull her out of me. But I felt stronger last week, like I could heal faster than before."

Spencer put a bandage on Emma's arm. "Your iron

was almost back to normal. It's probably just your diet and the addition of iron pills."

"You mentioned it before. Emma told me you and the others felt it, too. Is it most songs, or just some songs?" Maggie said.

"No, just the one song," Emma said. "I didn't feel anything like it at the concert Thursday."

He sighed. "It happened to us, too. When she sings 'Least of My Kind.' Keon didn't notice, but it freaked Tick out. We haven't talked about it since, but I think it has something to do with how we relate to the song."

"And her voice." Maggie drummed her fingers on the table. "Like when she yelled at the house."

Maggie left the room, leaving Spencer to clean up the supplies and Emma to rest. Two minutes later, she appeared with Clare beside her.

"Can you sing for us?" Maggie sat down again next to Emma.

"What?" Clare frowned. "I guess I can. What do you want me to sing?"

"'Least of My Kind'," Maggie answered.

Clare looked at the others in the room, but her eyes lingered on Spencer. He walked to her and wrapped his arm around her shoulder.

"It's fine. Maggie just wants to see something. Don't stop until Emma or she tells you to." He kissed her cheek and took a step back.

Clare shook her arms and patted her leg, creating a beat. With a deep breath, she began.

"Covered in dirt and mud, aching and spitting blood,

Cursing, you stir to rise and groan."

His wolf took notice from the first note from her mouth. He could feel it right beside him in his mind, looking through his eyes. No doubt, the color of his eyes changed.

He looked over at his sister. Her eyes were now a golden color. He remembered the first time her eyes changed. The night their father was murdered by a lone hunter, her wolf began to push through. Ethan found her covered in blood, holding their dad. A disassembled body lay twenty feet away. Her eyes didn't return to normal for two days.

Clare hit the chorus and his wolf pushed for control. His wolf wanted out. He looked down at his arms, hair getting longer, his hands changing. Emma's eyes glowed like never before. She clutched the table.

"Don't stop," she said.

He pulled his wolf back when he saw Clare's wide eyes, her voice faltering. She sang the last word in the chorus, and a loud snap caused him to jump.

"Stop. Stop singing." Maggie said.

Emma held part of the table in her hand. She'd snapped a chunk off at the end. Clare stopped singing, and Spencer's wolf retreated with a huff.

"I'm so sorry." Clare placed her hands over her mouth.

"You're sorry? I broke the table."

"That's crazy. You just broke the table." Spencer pulled the piece out of her hand.

"Do you think you can fix it?" Emma frowned.

"No. And I don't want to. I think I'll frame it. I'll name it Power of the Carrier."

"Ass." Emma hit his stomach with the back of her hand half-heartedly.

"I'm serious. I'm impressed. My sister is a badass."

Maggie laughed. "Did you just figure that out?"

He smiled and looked over at Clare. She stood backed up to the counter behind her, her hands still over her mouth. His arms wrapped around her.

"Are you okay?"

"No. What's wrong with me?"

"Nothing is wrong with you."

"Yes, yes there is. Last night and then just now. You were sprouting hair. Her eyes glowed."

"I don't think there is anything wrong. Just something new. We'll figure it out together."

"I think it's time you call your grandmother," Maggie chimed in.

"What?"

"There has to be a reason she purchases special items from me."

~

Clare

Clare paced upstairs in her temporary room, clutching the phone. She needed to talk to her ammachi. Could she have the answers to Clare's strange ability? No explanation could ease her mind. If she were honest, she'd rather not know.

But she couldn't go on this way. Everything felt out of control. And she didn't like not having some semblance of control. She looked down. The skull socks on her feet said 'Bad Bitch.' She took a deep breath. That's why she bought them, right?

"I am a bad bitch," she said to herself. "Nothing can keep me down."

She pushed the call button and waited for her ammachi to answer.

"Clare. I've been waiting for your call." She sounded pleased.

"Sorry, I haven't called much this past week. I've been busy."

"You're a working adult. Of course, you're busy, though you should find time to call me more often."

"I will. I promise. But I kind of have a question."

"What sort of question?"

"Why do you order stuff from Maggie?"

"Maggie sells a particular spice that I have difficulty finding here."

"What do you do with the spice?"

"I put it in tea. Why are you asking these questions?"

"Um...I got overwhelmed yesterday and screamed. The sound hurt everyone's ears."

"Your voice does carry."

"They were all on the floor."

"I see. Has this happened before?"

"No. But...there's something else. When I sing a specific song, it causes people to...change."

"How much has Maggie told you?"

"About witches or werewolves?"

"I think it's best if I talk to you in person. I'll call you when I'm in Savannah. I love you, dear. Try not to yell too much until you talk to me."

The phone beeped, signaling the end of the call. Clare stared down at her phone. Why is her ammachi coming here? What does she need to tell her in person that she can't tell her over the phone?

She looked back at her socks. "I am a bad bitch. I can't forget it."

~

Spencer

Spencer stood in the living room doorway, looking up toward the stairs. Clare had been upstairs for over an hour. She needed her space, but that was the last thing he wanted to give her. For now, he squashed the urge to charge up the stairs and contented himself with staring at them instead.

Maggie wasn't sure how Clare's grandmother related to the supernatural, but she was positive that it affected Clare. Why did it take so long for Clare to discover it?

He shook his head. Maybe it had to do with her proximity to so many supernatural creatures. Did her family keep themselves away from the supernatural? It's almost impossible for anyone. Supernatural beings freely integrated within human society.

Standing and staring didn't help. Maggie and Emma left when Clare went upstairs. Clare would need to return to Maggie's house soon to grab more of her stuff. It could be an excellent excuse to talk to her and see her.

He rubbed the back of his neck. Why did finding his mate have to be so hard?

The quiet settled around him. The old house didn't make a sound, even with his weight against the door frame. How much time did he stay in this house alone? Why did he feel lonelier now than before?

A soft sound trickled down the stairs. The strumming of a guitar. He'd know it anywhere. Her guitar was one of the few items she brought with her last night.

He couldn't keep his feet glued to the floor any longer and was halfway up the stairs when he realized he'd started moving. He listened to the music which floated through the door. He recognized the song. One they didn't play, but she must like it, 'Help, I'm Alive' by Metric. She began singing, and the words hit him hard. He felt sadness with a dash of fear as he listened. Were these her emotions?

He softly turned the doorknob and peeked inside. She sat on a chair next to the bed, facing the window. The electric guitar didn't make much noise without the amp, but his enhanced hearing heard it perfectly.

He padded quietly into the room. She strummed and sang with her eyes closed, face toward the sun pouring through the window, warming her. His heart beat faster. The gorgeous glow on her face, her full lips moving, and how she swayed to the rhythm called to him. How in the world did he deserve a mate with such intelligence, talent, drive, and beauty?

The song ended, and she draped herself over her guitar. Her eyelids opened and she stared out the window. A small smile graced her lips, and he wished she'd look at him that way.

"Clare," he whispered. He didn't want to startle her.

She turned toward him. Her dark brown eyes looked deep and clear, the perfect place to drown.

"How are you feeling?" He kneeled in front of her.

She smiled. "Better. I just needed to remember something."

"What's that?"

Her toes wiggled against his knees. He looked down. Her skull socks shook back and forth. The words "Bad Bitch" were written below each skull.

"Are you saying your socks helped you out?"

He felt himself grin like an idiot when she laughed.

"I'm glad something could remind you of who you are." He leaned forward and snuck a kiss, but she pulled him back for another before he could escape.

"Thank you."

"For what?"

"For giving me a safe place to stay. And for being here for me. And for being you."

"You're welcome."

She leaned back in her chair and strummed the guitar. "Want to play together?"

"Sure. I have a couple of amps in my room if you want to use one."

"Maybe." She stood up and offered him her hand. "Lead the way."

Chapter 19

Clare

Her heart felt full. She could handle what life threw at her. If Spencer stayed beside her, she decided she could make it through. She was a bad bitch, after all.

Spencer's room was to the right at the top of the stairs. A white and navy striped area rug hid much of the hardwood floor. The walls were a steel blue, with one darker than the others. Two dressers sat side by side across from a low standing queen bed. In one corner sat his guitar in a holder next to an amp and an old kitchen chair. Framed band posters filled the walls, except for one that looked like an album, and another of lightning over a cityscape.

"Look at you. An accent wall." She pointed to the darker wall.

"Yeah. I can't take too much credit. It's only darker because I punched a hole in it and picked the wrong paint color after fixing it."

"Why'd you punch the wall?"

"It was right after my dad died."

"Oh. I'm sorry to bring that up."

He shrugged, pulled a metal folding chair out from beside the dressers, and placed it beside the other one. He offered her the kitchen chair, then a cord for her guitar, and plugged it into the amp. He pulled another amp from his closet and set it up. Only then did he pick up his guitar and sit.

She watched him tune the instrument, especially how his nimble hands worked the pegs. His long, callused fingers felt surprisingly good on her skin when they kissed. She wondered if he liked how her own callused fingers felt.

Sitting beside Spencer and playing the guitar calmed Clare down. The energy between the two of them filled the air. She watched as he played along with her, a soft smile on his face, his eyes glancing her way. Her chest never tightened like this for her old boyfriend. Sure, she would be nervous, but with Spencer she felt excited, too. She didn't think falling in love with someone else would feel so different.

Her strumming faltered.

"Are you okay?" Spencer slowed down the rhythm.

"I'm fine. Sorry." She smiled at him. Was this feeling love?

Here in this room, in this house, she felt like she belonged. Spencer gave her space here. She could spread out. Even as a guest, he set aside an area in the study just for her and cleaned off a shelf in the refrigerator for any foods she wanted to keep.

Maggie welcomed her into her house, but it was always a temporary arrangement. Her space was confined to one room with an area in the kitchen. Maggie's home possessed a constant energy buzzing about the place, even with no one home. Spencer's home felt calm, even with everyone milling about.

All the looks he'd given her over the past week, the way he sat next to her on Keon's couch, and the unconscious way he touched her came back to her. It was love. A desire for her that won't go away. She'd be lying to herself if she didn't find the idea appealing. Now, as they built a song with each other, creating harmonies with one another, she couldn't stop the itch to touch him from bubbling up inside her.

But if she bonded with him and left, he'd fall apart, right? It sounded like something she wouldn't wish on her worst enemy. After such a short time, she couldn't imagine him not being in her life. She wasn't even sure how to create that bond with him. Should she take that chance and form that bond?

The tune they played became alive between them. The two of them creating a new song without words or interruptions made her heart beat harder. She'd never been so in sync with anyone before.

Her eyes glanced at him once more, her fingers played on instinct. His eyes caught hers. The stare drew her in, and she felt powerless to look away. She didn't want to look away.

"Clare?"

"Yes."

"You stopped playing."

"Huh?" she looked down. "You did too."

She leaned over and placed a hand on his cheek. "I don't want to play anymore."

She leaned her guitar against the wall, then moved his into the holder. She straddled his empty lap and sank into a kiss. The last of the tension from her shoulder melted away when he wrapped his arms around her waist. Her hands gripped his hair, and she increased the pressure of their mouths. She wanted to fuse with him.

His hands slipped under her shirt, electrifying her skin. A firm hand held her against his chest as the other dipped in her pants and grabbed her bottom. She pulled away for a second and stared into his now golden eyes. The intensity drew her in again, and she nibbled down his neck and sucked where it met his shoulders, marking him as hers as a wild fury of emotions overcame her. She pulled his shirt off, exposing a silver necklace and a crescent moon tattoo on his arm.

The round charm showed the head of a wolf howling. Her hand traveled to the moon tattoo, where she traced the outline. Inside of the crescent stood the outline of several evergreen trees. She leaned forward and kissed the moon.

The ink flamed the fire in her belly. Her arms snaked behind him where she scratched down his back and bit into his shoulder. His moan alone could make her wet between her legs, but how he kneaded her ass and bit her lips already guaranteed a pair of soaked underwear.

He lifted her and moved to the bed. She bounced

where she landed and found his slim frame hovering over her, his legs on either side of her hips.

"Are you sure this is what you want?" His question came out almost as a growl.

"Yes. I'm more than sure."

She pushed forward and met his mouth. The frantic kiss between the two set her heart ablaze. She bit his bottom lip when he pulled away.

"I don't want desperate. I want to treat you right." He nuzzled her neck, licking down to her shoulder. His hands pulled her shirt off before she could stop him. "We can go slow," he murmured against her skin.

Kisses traced down to her breast, still covered in whatever bra she threw on when she woke up. His lips danced around the fabric, leaving her nipples aching to be touched.

Callused fingertips grazed her sides. She arched into his mouth and moaned when his teeth scraped her skin. Her heart pounded, and her mind felt fuzzy. He moved so slowly. Twinges of need pulsed between her legs. She wanted to beg him to go faster and also to go slower. His touch was something to savor, but now it drove her insane.

Her pants and underwear slid off her body. Spencer stood over her at the foot of his bed, shirtless, with his lean muscles stretched down his arms. His body looked like he wasn't a stranger to the gym. He looked at her, eyes aglow and nostrils flaring. Slowly, he kneeled and ran his hands up her thighs. Those fingers gripped her hips and pulled her down to the edge of the bed. He stared into her eyes when he placed each of her legs over his shoulders. She watched him lick his lips and lower his head. He kissed her stomach. She tried to wiggle her hips, but he held her in place. A soft kiss to her mound followed, and only then did he lazily lick at her aching clit.

The sounds she made at first contact surprised her. Who knew she could make such a needy and sexy sound? The noise escaped with each pass of his tongue, so she covered her mouth.

"Hmm." The vibrations of his voice made her eyes roll in the back of her head. "Don't cover your sound. I want to hear you. I want to hear how you feel when I touch you."

He sucked on her clit and she squeaked with pleasure. The fingers of one hand traced around the entrance to her center. She bucked at the sensation. The pressure of his tongue increased, and he plunged a finger into her wetness. Her hands gripped the sheets to keep from jumping out of her skin. His touch, his tongue, activated the nerves all the way to her nipples and down to her toes. She arched her back and ground into his face. How on earth could anyone make her feel this good?

A second finger joined the first. His other hand stopped her grinding. She whimpered, but he changed how he licked her in a way which made her pant. His fingers inside of her stroked her. Need built up like a dam ready to burst. The small bundle of nerves he controlled was stretched thin, ready to snap. He stopped and kissed her nub.

"Don't stop," she breathed.

She palmed his head and pushed it back down.

"Faster."

"Yes, ma'am."

He followed her instructions. Within seconds she climaxed. Her voice rang out in the room. Her nipples tingled, and Spencer's tongue lapped up the last of her vibrations. He pulled his fingers out, only to lick her slit.

"You taste so good." He moaned, still licking and kissing her vulva.

His golden eyes looked up at hers. A goofy grin appeared on his face and she couldn't help but smile back.

"Did you have fun?" she asked. Her breathing slowed.

"Absolutely." He rested his head on one of her thighs and watched her. "Can I keep you?"

"It's a definite possibility. Would I get to keep you in return?"

"You already have me." He kissed the inside of the opposite thigh, then climbed up to lie beside her. "You've had me since I first laid eyes on you."

"It's a big responsibility."

"Maybe. I cook and clean. I can play the guitar. I have a house and a job. Would you like references?"

She kissed his nose. "Maybe. Right now, you have way too many clothes on."

She planted kisses around his face and undid his belt. His hand stilled hers.

~

Spencer

Spencer leaned his head against Clare's. Her kisses ceased when he stopped her from completely opening his pants. He hated this moment. With her in his arms, all he wanted to do was to complete the bond between them. But to do so at that moment would be unfair to her.

"We can't. Not how I want. Probably not how you want." He whispered, but the wolf inside of him howled.

"What? Why? Is there something wrong with…you?" She looked down at his hand holding hers, hovering over his groin.

"No." He huffed a laugh through his nose. "Everything is functional there. It's just…"

He looked into her brown eyes and hoped for understanding. "Engaging in full intercourse will complete the bond between us."

"Oh." Her eyes widened.

"I don't want to decide for you."

"But we could do what we just did, and that doesn't…."

"Yeah. It's weird. I don't exactly understand it, but vaginal sex and anal sex both complete the bond between two people."

"What about lesbians?"

"I'm not sure. I think it has to do with the transfer of fluids between genitals. I've never asked any lesbian werewolves. And it's not covered in the books written on the subject."

"So, we can have all the oral sex and hand jobs as long as we don't exchange...fluids."

"Yeah."

"We made sex sound kind of weird." Her laugh echoed in the room.

The sound caused his chest to tighten. Weird sounding or not, he wanted to cement their connection and drown in her. He pulled her to him and kissed her. He never wanted to leave her side.

"I don't want to force you to decide when you're not ready."

"I don't want to leave you waiting forever."

"I have forever to wait for you."

She averted her eyes and then pulled him in for a hug. He hugged her tight in turn and breathed her in. His hands caressed her soft skin. Her face pressed hard into his shoulder, and her calloused fingers dug deep into his back. The smell of sandalwood and buttercream engulfed him. He could only hold her tight as his wolf whimpered and howled in his head. He wanted more. But he couldn't push her, no matter how much he wanted an answer and her love.

Chapter 20

Clare

Clare slept alone that night. She tossed and turned, thinking about her time with Spencer, only getting a few hours' sleep. She wasn't sure how she felt. Did she feel love or lust? Was it real or magically manufactured?

Spencer made her breakfast the next day. He didn't bring up the conversation from the day before, but he didn't miss any opportunity to run his fingers down her cheek or place a hand on the small of her back.

Ethan arrived to take her to Maggie's house to pick up more of her things. He arrived just in time. Her lust for Spencer pushed all rational thought from her head, and she almost pulled him upstairs on multiple occasions.

Ethan didn't talk much to her. But he offered to listen to her if she needed to talk to someone. She wanted to talk to someone she trusted, but who could she talk to about the supernatural?

Three cars lined up in Maggie's driveway next to hers when they arrived. Clare didn't recognize any of them.

"We have a few people trying to boost the security here. And I believe there is someone here that wants to see you."

Clare opened the door and stepped out. "Are you not going to stay?"

"I'll be back in a few hours. You can take your car to Spencer's when you're ready to leave." Ethan smiled as he backed out of the driveway.

She lazily waved to the rear of his car. Who wants to see her?

Clare walked around the house to enter through the back door. She saw Maggie at the river and Sylvia near the fence opposite the driveway. Others she didn't recognize all scattered something in the wind. Maggie stood near the river, her hand waving high above her. Particles dropped from her moving hand. What was she spreading?

A few people in the yard nodded to her, but none came to greet her. She made her way inside, and the smell of curry hit her. At the stove stood a dark brown woman in a green sari, stirring a pot. She turned and smiled at Clare, her gray hair the only thing about her which hinted at her age.

"What are you doing here?" Clare rushed to her ammachi's side and hugged her tightly.

"I told you I was coming. You should pay attention more often." She patted her back. "Now, back up. I'm cooking for Maggie and her friends."

Clare stepped back and stared at her ammachi. Why did she come to Savannah?

"What are you staring at? Don't you know how to make curry?"

"What are you doing here?"

"I am helping. Maggie tells me someone wants to steal magic. So, I help as I can."

"How do you know about magic?"

She reached over and patted Clare on her cheek. "I am magic."

"What?"

"I am a Siren. I fell in love and left my choir."

"What? Choir?"

"That's what a group of Sirens is called. Like a flock of birds, but a choir of Sirens."

"And you are here to help? But you're like 70 or 80. Why don't I know how old you are?"

"I am close to 200."

"What? Does appachin know?"

She nodded. "But I told him years after I married him. I don't recommend waiting that long."

Clare pulled a stool from the island and sat near the stove. "What exactly is a Siren? Do you really sing to bring men to their death?"

A laugh rang through the room. "No. We sang to attract men to have babies. All females born from sirens are automatically sirens as well. Males do not possess the same power. They are either thrown back into the waves or taken ashore and placed at a home to be adopted."

"Wow. Did you ever throw a male child away? Do you have siren girl children?"

"I have two daughters. They still live off the coast of

south India with the choir. They were near a hundred when I met your appachin. And no, I never threw away a male child. Your father is my only male."

"Do you turn into a mermaid? I read somewhere that sirens and mermaids were the same."

Her ammachi laughed. "Not at all. Sirens sing like birds, therefore we can fly. We turn into bird women to travel. We once shared islands with our mermaid cousins. After human's technology flourished, they descended deep into the ocean, waiting for the humans to fall. My sisters rely on magic to remain in their natural habitat."

"Can I see you as a bird?" Clare asked with wide eyes.

"Not today, my little one."

"This is all so crazy. Why did you leave? How did you know it would work out with appachin?"

"I am magic. We just know love when it meets us. And nothing is guaranteed, but some things are worth the risk."

"Am I magic, too? Am I a siren?"

"No. You have the natural ability to sing well, but without the power of a siren. And based on what they said about your scream, you have a bit of magic, but you are not magic."

"What's the difference?"

"The difference? If magic disappears, I will disappear, but you will not. The scream will disappear, not you."

She frowned at her ammachi. "Is someone really trying to get rid of magic?"

"Maggie says they want to take all the magic for themselves."

"Are these the people that are attacking her?"

"They are the people who put a bounty on her head."

"A bounty?"

"After I spoke to you, I called Maggie. Then I visited a local choir off the coast of New Jersey and found the bounty information. She's worth five hundred-thousand."

"Damn. That's crazy. Wait, how many choirs are there?"

The older lady laughed. "As many as flocks of birds in the sky."

"And you are here to help?"

"Of course. My Clare is involved."

"I could just leave, and then you could leave."

"Would you leave your soul mate?"

Clare rubbed her face with her hands. "Maggie told you?"

"Yes. He sounds like a wonderful young man."

"Did she tell you he's a werewolf?"

"She did."

"Ugh." Clare pouted. "I haven't decided yet."

"What do you need to decide?"

"If I'm going to stay. If I'll be with him."

Her ammachi bopped her on the head. "What would you do otherwise?"

"Find someone else?"

She slowly stirred the curry, then lowered the heat and placed a lid on top. "Do you think you can walk away now that you've met him?"

Clare sighed. "No. But I don't really want to get more

involved with the supernatural."

"Your scream brought wolves to their knees. You cannot escape yourself."

Clare scrunched up her face. "I'm scared."

"We all are scared. It's what we do despite the fear that tells us who we are."

"I do like him," she whispered. "How do I know if it's love?"

"Does it pain you to be away from him now?"

She closed her eyes and took a deep breath. She felt lost without him close. Was that tightness in her chest a desire to be near him? She didn't know.

"Pay attention to how you feel when you see him next. That will be your answer."

"How long are you going to be here?"

"Until some of my sisters come. There are sirens all around the world, and we are all sisters. A choir off the coast of Hilton Head Island has agreed to help. Only you will be able to call them."

"There's another island near Hilton Head? And how can I call them?"

"Our islands are not detectable by man. And you can call them with this necklace. Rub the jade eye of the bird and say what you need."

She placed a small bird silhouette charm with a tiny jade eye around Clare's neck. Clare studied the charm.

"It's beautiful." Her head jerked up. "Wait. I thought sirens were Greek."

Her ammachi tried not to roll her eyes. "The sirens in the Mediterranean were well known and less discreet than the rest of us. We live all over the globe, and we all look different."

"How do you know if someone is a siren?"

"We just know. You'll know too. They will feel like me. Trust your instinct."

"Okay." She admired the charm some more. "Thank you for this."

"I only wish I could have told you sooner."

She hugged her ammachi. "I need to grab some more things. I'm staying at the pack house for now."

"Yes. Maggie doesn't think the fortifications will be done for a few more days. Of course, you might not come back at all."

Her eyes widened. "Ammachi!"

The laugh of bells followed Clare upstairs.

She didn't have much that she needed in the room where she'd lived in for a little over a month. More clothes, her laptop, her amp and pedals, and any toiletries she didn't grab the first time. The sad state of her room reminded her of what she left behind in Philadelphia. Of course, she had stuff in storage, but all in all, she couldn't be too disappointed. She left a toxic environment and found something new, even if it was scary. But should she be scared?

She placed her amp and two bags near the foot of the stairs. Her ammachi had a pile of naan on a plate and a large bowl of rice.

"It looks good."

"It's quick naan, so it won't be as good as homemade."

Clare took a bite of the bread on top of the stack. "It's good. Want me to call everyone inside to eat?"

"Yes."

"Ammachi…do you think it'd be okay if I stayed here forever? This was just supposed to be temporary. What if I stay indefinitely?"

"I'm happy if you are happy. Fate calls all of us in different ways and at different times. It's up to you how you answer."

Clare stayed at Maggie's with her ammachi until early afternoon. Her shoulders still felt tense even after her time with family. Something didn't feel right, but now she needed to think about work tomorrow. She drove her car to Spencer's, so she wouldn't need to rely on anyone else to drive her to work.

The outside of the brick house stood quiet before her. The light inside told her someone was home. She pulled her bags and amp out of her car and walked to the door. She might need a key at this rate, but today the door opened before she stepped on the porch. Spencer stood with the hall light shining behind him.

His lazy smile greeted her. "Welcome back."

The tightness in her shoulders melted away with one look at the man before her. The relief she felt at his presence surprised her. What she really wanted was to hug him.

"You look happy," he said as he took the amp from her hand.

"I didn't realize I was smiling." She walked past him and the door closed.

"You are. I love it when you smile."

Her heart beat loud in her chest. "I should put this upstairs."

She felt him walk behind her as she ascended the stairs and into her room.

They put down the stuff at the foot of the bed. She felt nervous. Could she really trust this feeling? Relief and happiness at the sight of Spencer. Could that be love? She wanted to jump into his arms when she was with him. There was no way she could walk away from him, and she knew it. Why was she still scared?

His brown eyes looked down at her and he rubbed the back of his neck. "Did you have a good time? You were gone for a while."

"Yes. My ammachi, my grandmother, was at Maggie's. She apparently knows all about the supernatural."

"Really? How?"

She stepped up to him and laced her arms around his waist, placing her ear over his heart. "I'll tell you later. Just let me stay like this for a bit."

His arms enclosed her, warming her from a chill she didn't realize she had, and kissed her head. This here, this was love. Soft and strong. Supportive and solid. She didn't know one touch could take away all her fears.

"I'm ready." She peered up at his face. "I'm ready."

Chapter 21

Spencer

Spencer looked down to see Clare's eyes peeking up at him. She stood on her tiptoes and kissed him. Her arms wrapped around his back and hooked on his shoulders. He leaned down to kiss her back. The soft feel of her lips on his turned his brain into jelly. He didn't know what she meant, but he'd stand behind her, whatever it was.

"Are you, now? You sure?" His thumb rubbed her cheek.

"Absolutely." She rubbed her nose against his.

"What does this mean? You're ready?"

She hummed against his cheek. "I'm ready. I love you. I've made my decision. I'm here to stay…if you'll have me."

Nothing prepared him for how he felt at that moment. Hope and love burned in his chest. He pulled her tightly to him and pressed her against the wall. His hands roamed her body as she electrified him with each brush of her fingers under his shirt.

She pulled away from his kiss and nibbled down his neck.

He moaned loudly when she sucked on his shoulder. "I don't want you to make a rash decision." His knees almost buckled when she wrapped a leg around his waist. "Do you want to sleep on it first?"

"I don't want to sleep on it. I want to sleep with you."

He grabbed her ass and picked her up, letting her wrap both legs around him. She pressed herself against his groin. It amazed him how fast she could make him erect.

"I don't want you to make your decision based on lust." He tried to stop her hips from moving.

She kissed him deeply. "I'm not. Seeing you in the doorway erased the tension in my shoulders. I smiled without knowing it. I thought about you all day and wished you were next to me. With one touch, my fears vanished. I'm in. I'm all in. If you want me to wait, I will. But I don't want to."

His heart pounded, and his wolf flooded his head with love and desire. "I won't be able to say no to you, will I?"

He swallowed her laugh and let go of her hips. Every part of him buzzed and tingled with her touch, her smell, and the sounds she made.

He walked her over to the bed and laid her down. Her dark hair splayed over the bed like a crown. He joined her on the mattress, kissed her, and ran his hands under her shirt, feeling her soft skin. She pulled his shirt over his head and threw it on the floor. His necklace landed on her shoulder. Her fingers gripped the charm, smiled, and kissed the round wolf medallion.

He teased down her neck and onto her shoulder. She arched her back toward him and he slipped his hand up her back and unclasp her bra. With one quick movement, he pulled her shirt and bra off together. Her nails bit into his shoulder blades. He loved the sensation of her marking him, even if that wasn't her intention.

A new necklace she wore caught his eye. He pulled it up to look at the small bird charm. Its stone's eye looked like it would wink at him at any moment.

Clare caressed his cheek. "My ammachi gave it to me."

"It suits you." He dropped the chain and kissed her neck under her chin while walking his hand up to caress one of her exposed breasts.

She moaned when he brushed her nipple with his thumb. He wanted to hear it again, so he gave it a light pinch. She surprised him with a little jerk under his body. Her hands slipped into his pants, but not before he could put his mouth over one of her delicious dark nipples. She gasped.

Her hands fumbled to unbutton his pants, but he wasn't concerned about that. "Slowly," he whispered. He wanted to take his time and give her as much pleasure as possible. He moved to the other nipple, running his tongue in circles around the tip. She arched into him again and gave up on his belt.

The tattoo on her arm needed attention. Musical notes circled her right arm. His thumb brushed against it, then he kissed each note he could, lifting her arm to kiss the rest. Her eyes widened when he turned her onto her stomach. Her back held two more tattoos, one of a tiny guitar on her left shoulder and the other of a small mandala between her shoulder blades. He traced the guitar with his finger before kissing the ink. Then traced the mandala with his tongue. His hands held her arms in place and felt her shiver under him. Her heart pounded so loud he could hear it. He slowed down the pace, nipped ever so slightly at her exposed neck. Finally, he kissed the center of the tattoo and let go.

She looked over her shoulder at him, eyes half closed and cheeks flushed. Her body rolled over under him. He looked down at her lovely naked half.

Her fingers reached up and outlined his own crescent moon tattoo. "Is this your only one?"

"It is." He settled a knee between her legs and sucked on her luscious tits. Her hands grabbed onto his hair. With each sound she made, his hard cock twitched. Yet, he hadn't finished giving her breasts the attention they deserved.

Each nipple needed praise and kisses. He sucked one nipple while he flicked the other with his thumb. Her groin rubbed against his leg with each stroke. He kissed each globe when she began to pant and nibbled down her side. Sounds hitched in her throat as he moved south along her body. Her pants slid off easily. He turned her over again and massaged her full bottom.

He lifted her rear and pushed her legs in so her ass stuck straight in the air. He leaned down and licked her cute pussy.

"Oh."

"You like that?" he asked.

"Yes."

He licked her again, then flicked her clit with his tongue. She wiggled her ass and pressed into his face.

Her moans grew louder, so he slowed down. He wanted to savor every second and drink her in. She whimpered at his reduced pace.

"Faster," she said.

His lips covered her clit, and he hummed.

"Faster." Her voice sounded strained.

"No. I want to take my time."

"I can't... please."

He licked her once more, then turned her on her back. "Such good manners."

A series of kisses traversed her body, pausing at her belly button, nipples, shoulders, each side of her neck, and each ear until he finally took her mouth with his again. Her arms pulled him tight against her. She slipped her hand into his pants and wrapped it around his stiff shaft.

He moaned in her mouth at the touch. She slid her hand up and down his dick. He couldn't stop himself from bucking in her hands. He pulled her closer and slipped his hand between her legs, rubbing her clit. She pressed against his hand and tightened her grip around him.

Feeling her wet slit, he slipped a finger inside. Then another. He pumped his fingers in and out, using his thumb to rub her bud. She shivered and shook in surprise.

She let go of his member and fumbled again with his pants. This time, she successfully pushed his pants down as far as she could. Her hands tried to push him on his back, but he held firm.

"Patience," he said.

A whine escaped her, followed by a gasp when he rubbed her bud faster and added a third finger. He moved his hand quicker and watched her head lean back. Her vagina tightened around his fingers and pulsed as she crescendoed. She kissed him when she returned to herself, and he slowly slipped out of her.

"My turn." Her voice caught him off guard.

He let her push him onto his back. She shimmed down his body and gave his hard penis a few pumps with her hands before she licked it from base to tip, causing him to shiver from head to toe. She licked him again, then took him into her mouth. Only half of him fit, but it still felt phenomenal. Each thrust she gave curled his toes.

She moved back to licking and kissing, then climbed on top of him. Through the haze, he reached over to his nightstand and opened the drawer. He fumbled around until he pulled out a condom. She pulled the package out of his hands and opened it. After rolling the condom over his dick, she clamped her knees around his hips. She licked his neck up to his ears, then kissed him while she lowered herself onto his cock.

"I wasn't ready," he croaked out.

She chuckled. "You'd better hurry."

She eased up and down, his dick sliding in and out of her wet vagina. He wanted to know if he filled her up, but he couldn't form words anymore.

His hands clasped her hips, helping the movement. He reached up and massaged one of her dangling breasts, and pulled her nearer to him. His mouth closed over the tip, and he licked the hard pebble. She mumbled something, then thrusted faster. The speed made him groan, and he felt his eyes roll to the back of his head.

One hand pinched a nipple while the other located her sensitive clit. He rubbed with one hand and pinched with the other. She slid herself faster and faster up and down his cock. He heard himself groan and growl. Abandoning her nipple, he pulled her down to claim her mouth.

He kissed and sucked on her tongue while flicking her nub. She panted into his mouth as her pussy clamped down on his dick, hitting her second climax. He burst shortly after.

She sprawled out on top of him, kissing his face and neck.

He rolled her onto the bed and nuzzled her neck. "You smell amazing," he murmured.

"You feel amazing."

"Would you like to feel more?" He waggled his eyebrows.

"Can you? Right now?"

"Absolutely."

~

Clare

Clare woke up a little after nine at night. The bed felt warm where Spencer had lain. Her body still tingled from his touch. She wished he'd stayed with her until she woke up. Maybe he'd come back soon. She wanted to hug him tight. The feelings she had for him grew over the last few hours.

Her stomach growled. That's right. She ate lunch with her ammachi and had nothing since. Instead of pulling on the clothes scattered on the floor, she opted to pull on pajamas. The house was quiet until she reached the bottom of the stairs. Voices came from the study. Maybe he wanted to eat as well. Once near the door, she could overhear the conversation.

"Erasing the bounty on Maggie requires more than magic to achieve," a woman's voice said. Clare thought it sounded like Sylvia.

"What do you mean?" Clare recognized Maggie's voice.

"A less than dignified person has agreed to help. In return, they may request a favor from me," Sylvia said.

"Sylvia, you have put yourself in a dangerous position." A man's voice said. She'd heard it before, but couldn't put a face to the sound.

Clare stepped backward. She really shouldn't listen in on this conversation.

Chapter 22

Spencer

Spencer woke to the sound of his phone's ring. His sensitive ears heard the low volume. He scrambled to find the phone in the mess of clothes on the floor.

"Hello?" he whispered.

"Spencer, where are you?" Emma asked.

"I'm upstairs in my house."

"You're not in your room."

"And?"

"Anyway, come downstairs. Ethan and Sylvia called a meeting. You're invited. Be in the study in ten minutes." Emma hung up the phone.

He looked over at the beauty who slept. He didn't want to leave her, ever. Downstairs wasn't far, but it would feel miles away. The bond between them felt strong already. It pulled at his chest, their hearts beating in sync. Once he gathered his clothes, he kissed her cheek and walked to his room. He made it downstairs with a shower within ten minutes.

The door to the study stood open. Ethan and Sylvia sat together across from the entrance. Isaiah, Emma, and Dylan, Sylvia's brother, who only showed up for the most serious decisions. Considering the last few months, why he hadn't showed up before now surprised Spencer.

"So, are we only waiting for Maggie?" he asked when he entered the room.

"Yes. She'll be here soon." Sylvia didn't look up from the notebook in her hand.

Ethan, Isaiah, and Emma stared at him as he took a seat next to Isaiah.

"Did you trick her?" Emma asked.

"No. I can't believe you'd say that." Spencer scowled at his sister. The joke didn't sit well with him.

"Does she know that she's now officially mated to you and what it means?" Isaiah crossed his arms with a frown.

"Yes. She knows. I told her." He growled after he spoke. What kind of person did they take him for?

"Who are you talking about?" Dylan's deep voice startled the group. He rarely spoke.

"Spencer's mate, Clare. She's the lady that's living with Maggie," Ethan answered.

"Ah. The Siren's grandchild."

"Siren's grandchild?" Spencer looked around the room.

"I guess it's her that didn't tell you everything." Ethan laughed. "I hear she only found out today. Don't be too hard on your mate."

"I just can't believe anyone would agree to have sex

with you." Emma pushed his leg with her foot.

"You'll have to think of something new. That's what you've said every time you hear about my sex life."

"It's a sister's job to tease." She lunged at him from her seat across from him, landing in a hug. "Congratulations."

"What are we congratulating him for?" Maggie walked into the room and sat in the chair Emma vacated.

"Spencer lured Clare into bed." Emma waggled her eyebrows.

Spencer pushed his sister off of him. "You make it sound terrible."

"Congratulations Spencer. Don't fuck it up." Maggie pulled Emma into the seat beside her.

Ethan cleared his throat. "Let's change the subject, now that we are all here."

Dylan pulled out a shimmering scroll and unfurled it. "I managed to get a copy of the bounty on Maggie. The only good thing is they want her alive. The downside is they must want information from her or to use her as bait."

The scroll showed a crude drawing of Maggie's face that changed between her blue hair and her now almost black hair. It was the only part of the picture with color. Her hair seemed to be the defining feature which cleared up the misunderstanding of why the last hunter went after Clare. The flyer gave her shop's address and stated she could only do 'old-fashioned magic.'

"Old-fashioned magic? I'll show them old-fashioned." Maggie flipped off the scroll.

"I've never heard magic called 'old-fashioned' before," Emma said.

Dylan rolled up the scroll. "It's an old-fashioned phrase, for lack of a better term. Now you'll hear it called slow magic or ritual magic."

"What can we do about the bounty on Maggie?" Emma asked.

"Erasing the bounty on Maggie requires more than magic to achieve." Sylvia enunciated more than usual.

"What do you mean?" Maggie leaned forward.

"A less than dignified person has agreed to help. In return, they may request a favor from me." Sylvia grimaced and looked away from the group.

"Sylvia, you have put yourself in a dangerous position," Ethan said. "What kind of favor would they ask of you in return?"

"That is yet to be determined and none of your business until I say so." Her glare sent Ethan shrinking in his chair. "Besides, one does what one must for family."

"You can't do that for me. Let me owe the favor. It's for me, after all," Maggie begged.

"It's already done. By midnight, they will erase the bounty as if fulfilled. The one who posted the bounty will not know for at least a week. It gives us time to plan."

"Do we know where the bounty came from, other than Cernunnos?" Spencer asked. Not many people knew about the data stolen from the complex in South Carolina. He didn't have access to it and couldn't bring himself to ask if it could help them now.

"The location to bring the bounty is not listed in the

data we acquired from Cernunnos. It is suspiciously in the middle of the three remaining locations in the United States." Sylvia waved her hand, and a holographic map appeared showing the location.

"Woah." Spencer couldn't stop himself. Sometimes, the magic performed by the coven members caught him off guard.

"We will send a small group to scout the area." Ethan tapped the holograph, and it zoomed in closer to the location.

Spencer wasn't always invited to these meetings and didn't know how often they used this magic. Seeing a werewolf interact with the magic map short-circuited his brain. Could he also control someone's magic? It's not something he'd ever heard about.

"Three groups of three will survey the area for a week. Sylvia and I discussed who we wanted to be team leaders. Isaiah, Dylan, and Spencer." Ethan smiled at Spencer. "Though now I think we should take Spencer off the list."

"Why?" He'd never been asked to be a team leader for a mission, and now Ethan didn't want him.

"You have a new mate bond. It's best to stay together for now."

"I think Sally or Zara would be good options," Maggie suggested.

"All options will be considered." Sylvia drummed her fingers on the arm of her chair.

"For now, Isaiah and Dylan, think about who you want on your team. Remember, Maggie and Emma have to stay here for now. Sylvia and I will discuss the third team." Ethan stood, signaling the end of the meeting.

"So, I no longer need a bodyguard, right?" Maggie's face lit up.

"No. Wait a few more days." Sylvia stood and squeezed Maggie's shoulder.

Maggie's face fell, but she didn't move from the spot. Everyone filed out of the room except Maggie, Emma, and Spencer. He smiled to himself then. For once, he wasn't asked to help the pack. He never thought he'd be excited about not helping.

"It feels weird not being asked to travel for the pack." Emma looked around. "It's like something is missing."

"You can't go because we need your blood. Muahahaha." Maggie shared her best Dracula laugh.

"Shut it. You know you want to go, too." Emma pushed her away.

"I do want to go. But not closer to the enemy. I need a vacation. Away from the shop and the coven."

"I feel like I'm on vacation." Spencer stood and smiled at them. "I never thought I'd be happy staying behind. I'm going to go...um...vacation."

He grinned wide enough to show his canines and pranced to the door. After all, his mate was only steps away.

"Ew, gross." Emma made a retching sound. "Try to keep the noise down."

A feeling in his chest took him to the kitchen, where Clare sat eating an apple. The smile she gave him made him weak in the knees. He straddled her lap and sat holding her in a hug. One arm rubbed his back. She kept eating with her other arm.

"I thought you'd be heavier," she said while chewing. "How was your meeting?"

"How did you know about the meeting?"

She kissed his cheek. "I might have almost interrupted looking for you. And as tempting as it was to eavesdrop, I heard Maggie's aunt and left. Her smile never quite reaches her eyes."

"Do you want something more than an apple?" He stood up with a laugh.

"Yes, please."

Chapter 23

Spencer

Spencer stared at Clare's sleeping figure. She fell asleep in his arms, and he couldn't stop admiring her. The weekend ended up a slow one. He'd forgotten how nice it felt to have nothing to do.

Of course, he never liked it before. Staying still reminded him of all he'd lost. He never knew his mom. His dad died when he was 18. Emma went off to vet school, and he tried to find something, anything, to do.

His life slowly centered around the pack. The enclosure fell under his care as well as the house his father left him and his sister. Even with a job and the band, it didn't keep away the memories. When Maggie asked him to deliver something from her, he immediately accepted. At first, the drives gave him too much time to think. After a while, the silence helped him heal, but he didn't slow down.

The woman beside him nuzzled into his side. Now, he found something better to fill his time.

Her scent already permeated everything in his room. He breathed the sweet smell of sandalwood and buttercream. He tucked her against his chest and fell asleep.

~

Clare

Clare untangled herself from Spencer after her alarm went off. He slept soundly while she navigated the dark room to find the door. She clutched her chest every time she felt the tug of her connection with Spencer. Work sounded less appealing than usual, knowing he wouldn't be beside her.

With a shake of her head, she tiptoed back into his room to kiss his forehead. His moan at her touch made her knees feel weak. Staying in bed with a gorgeous guy sounded much better than working, though not as practical.

The tug at her chest tightened the further she drove away from him. A wave of sadness overcame her as she pulled into the parking lot. Was this his emotion? He mentioned they would eventually have an emotional connection, but she didn't think it would happen so quickly.

Her phone dinged, and she pulled it up. "Where are you?" Spencer texted.

A smile spread across her face. She messaged back, "I had to go to work. I didn't want to wake you up."

"I want to kiss you before you leave. Always. Wake

me up next time."

An intense love bloomed within her. "I will." She added a heart and then walked into work wearing a goofy grin.

~

Spencer

Spencer had a hard time concentrating on his own job. Clare's emotions hit him like a ton of bricks every few hours. Some he didn't understand, and others filled him with a strong need to drive to her workplace and kill someone. He never knew that engineering could be so emotional. Why would anyone choose a job like that?

Under all the emotions that came across their connection, he felt love. It worried him that the love felt weak. Of course, it existed, so he should be grateful. Only what ifs trickled into his thoughts. She could change her mind at any time and would never truly know his pain. He rubbed the back of his neck. No, she wouldn't do that. He felt her love. Love grows. He would feel it more the stronger their connection becomes, right?

He had to be the only person to doubt someone's love after a bond. He could feel it. He just wanted it to be stronger. What a selfish thought. With a deep breath, he searched for that underlying love. The delicate feeling brushed against this heart. Love so fragile, he feared breaking it.

With a sigh, he made his decision. He could help grow the love, strengthen it. He wanted them to have a love built with trust. Home suddenly felt too far away.

~

Roderic

Andre rushed into Roderic's office without knocking. "I have news."

Roderic raised an eyebrow at his second in command. "I hope it's worth barging in without knocking."

"Someone took down the bounty. Last night around midnight. I'm working on tracing who canceled it." Steam practically poured out of his nose.

"Hmm..." He turned and looked out the window of the office. The sea of trees outside ran down into a small valley. A small lake looked picture-perfect at the bottom. "Don't worry about it. It's unexpected, but we can use it to our advantage."

"Are you serious?" His hands curled into fists at his side.

Roderic turned back. "Yes. There is no harm in moving up our timeline. Notify Gunther. Plan 'Snag the Witch' is in full play."

"Are you sure Gunther is adequate for this job?"

"He will get the book. Or he will die trying."

"And the girl? Do you really think she'll talk?"

Roderic sat in his chair. He enjoyed the leather smell. "Pain is a great motivator."

Chapter 24

Maggie

"It's too quiet." Maggie sat upside down on the couch.

"It's always too quiet here, unless it's a full moon night." Emma popped some popcorn into her mouth.

"Yes, but that's not what I mean." Maggie's feet kicked back and forth on the back of the couch. "It's quiet everywhere. Here. The shop. My house. The car."

"You're on edge. Just enjoy not being attacked for a while."

"How long do you think it will last?"

"Based on what Sylvia and Clare's siren grandmother said, they probably won't notice the bounty's been canceled for at least a week. So, I think we have until next weekend."

Maggie rolled on her stomach and slid onto the floor. "I want to take the battle to them. I want to take care of this once and for all."

Emma frowned at her and continued to eat.

"I just want to relax. I've never not felt safe until now.

It's terrible."

"Do you think Sylvia's still lying about that book?"

"Yes. Even if she's not, we don't have a good way of convincing Cernunnos we don't have it."

"Maybe that's what we need to focus on, convincing them we don't have that stupid book."

"Have any ideas on how to do that?"

"Send them a cease-and-desist letter from our witchy lawyer? Dear assholes. We don't have that book. Please go away. Signed Jesi, the witch lawyer."

"Maybe I should go. Convince them we don't have it. Maybe they'll let me go." Maggie laughed. "Just kidding. They'll probably just kill me or use me in an experiment."

"Can you make a puppet to look like you?"

Maggie's eyes widened. "That's dangerous magic. I wouldn't even try it."

"I wonder why they are so intent on capturing you?"

"Well, to be honest, everyone wants to be near me. I'm amazing, hilarious, and talented."

"Is that what you tell yourself?" Emma threw popcorn at Maggie. "I mean, you look hilarious. You don't smell terrible. Maybe they want you for a circus."

"Spoken like a true best friend." She sat up and sniffed the air. "What's that smell?"

Emma laughed. "I wondered how long it would take you. I think Clare's grandmother is cooking."

"Ms. Gayatri is the best. I wish she lived down here. Think we could convince her to move?"

~

Spencer

Spencer walked into his house, and a delicious smell hit him. His nose led him straight to the kitchen. An older woman stood at the stove in a light blue sari, stirring a pot. Clare stared over her shoulder. The two women heavily favored each other, yet the stare from the older lady knocked him back a step. The power he felt just from a look intimidated him.

Clare spotted him and skipped into his arms with a kiss. "I'm glad you're here. Come. Meet my ammachi. Ammachi, this is Spencer. Spencer, this is Gayatri Anand, my grandmother."

Sweat started dripping down the small of his back. "Hello Ms. Anand. Pleased to meet you."

Gayatri's eyes softened and she smiled. Few lines appeared on her face. The only indication of her age appeared in her gray hair. She could pass as an older sister, or maybe Clare's mother.

"It's a pleasure to meet you, young man. I have heard good things about you from Clare and Maggie."

"What brings you to Savannah?" He held onto Clare lightly, not wanting to let go, yet fearing a negative reaction from her grandmother.

"No one told you?" She chuckled. "I'm a Siren, here to help my Clare's new family."

"Right." His hand tightened around her waist.

Clare leaned into his ear. "Sorry, I forgot to tell you."

He smiled at her. "It's been a little busy."

"Ammachi is going home in a few hours. But she wanted to cook for us. And Maggie."

"Emma's here, too."

"Really? How do you know?"

"Her car is outside. And I can smell her."

"You can smell others even with my delicious sauce cooking? You have a good nose." Gayatri walked over and bopped his nose. "Dinner is ready. Set the table. I will go find Maggie."

She floated out of the room.

"Is she walking or rolling?"

Clare laughed. "She always walks like that. So smooth. I used to try to do the same. I fell so many times, though I can do it now. Not as much fun as it looks."

"She's a bit scary. I never really considered Sirens. I wonder if they all give off that aura."

"She's not scary! She's sweet and wonderful."

"That's because she's your grandma. You didn't see the look she gave me when I walked in. I almost walked back out."

Clare pulled him into a hug, her head on his shoulder. "But you stayed."

With Clare in his arms, his entire body relaxed. Their hearts beat as one as they swayed in place.

"I can feel you when I'm at work," she whispered.

"I can feel you, too. What made you so mad today?"

A groan filled the room. "My boss signed a document for release, but apparently didn't review it and blamed everyone for his actions. I wanted to hit him."

"I could tell. I had to convince myself not to come help."

Her hand stroked his head. "I'm sorry. It's going to take a while to get used to this."

"I hope we never get used to it. I want it to always feel new."

"So sappy. You gonna write a love song now?"

"Yep. I'll sing it to you at our next concert."

~

Maggie

"My contact has successfully canceled the contract," Sylvia said.

Maggie didn't quite relax with the update. "Can I go home now?"

Sylvia, Ethan, Maggie, and Emma sat in the study at Spencer's home. Sylvia and Ethan looked at each other and frowned.

"Ugh. That's a no," Maggie sighed. "I haven't slept in my own bed in four nights. How much longer do we have to wait?"

"Forever if we have to." Sylvia's deadpan expression sunk Maggie's hopes.

"Has anyone devised a plan to convince them we don't have this book they want?" Emma chimed in.

"Our coven is one of the oldest and strongest in the country. Even if we convince the hunters of the truth, they may very well go after another coven, one unprepared to fight. I do not want a destroyed coven on my hands." Sylvia pursed her lips and somehow sat straighter.

"You and Ethan have obviously been planning something. Do you want to let us in on your plans?" Maggie crossed her arms over her chest. She didn't care how much she pouted at the moment.

"We plan to form an army," Ethan said.

"What?" Emma jumped to her feet. "How?"

Sylvia cleared her throat. "We have allies. It's time we called upon them for help. If they find this book, then the whole of the supernatural community will be destroyed. Not just those who use magic for good, but those for evil as well."

"Are you saying we will work with evil forces?" Maggie couldn't stop her mouth from dropping. "How would we even contact them?"

"My contact from before has not disappeared."

"Sylvia, I'm sure the others agree that we are surprised you have such a contact." Ethan gazed intently at her.

She raised an eyebrow and her chin. The two didn't break eye contact or blink. It reminded Clare of two cats staring each other down.

"As much as I want to continue watching this strange display of pride between the two of you, when do you think this army of ours will be ready?" Emma snapped her fingers between the two leaders. "And do you expect us to attack first?"

"We're still gathering information." Ethan swatted at Emma to stop. "The data from the last attack has proved invaluable. But that doesn't mean it's one hundred percent accurate. Things change. We still need to confirm some of our findings."

"You're not going to show us the findings, are you?" Maggie asked.

"You are being hunted. The less you know, the better." Sylvia stood. "You can move back in a week if there are no attacks."

Sylvia left with Maggie making faces in silent protest. Ethan patted her on the head and exited the room as well.

"There are worse places to stay," Emma reminded her.

"It's just in the middle of nowhere, and it takes so long to get to the shop."

"Would you rather be a sitting duck?"

"I'd rather be a duck in general." She stood up and waddled like a duck out of the room.

"That's more of a penguin walk. You need a more exaggerated stride."

Chapter 25

Clare

The band practiced at Spencer's house for the next week. Keon wasn't happy about the prospect as he had more equipment to carry, however they were performing for the pack the night after the full moons. Ethan liked to have parties several times a year, including the beginning of the school year.

Having not practiced since the concert, Keon insisted they practice Tuesday, Wednesday, and Thursday, plus a long practice on Saturday. Keon also insisted on switching up the set list, making practice last longer, with the ensuing bickering between the other three regarding the list. She thought she'd have more time to spend alone with Spencer now, but she couldn't exactly argue with Keon. They needed to practice.

When she got home on Thursday, she changed her clothes and grabbed her guitar. Spencer cleaned out the garage, and most of the band's gear stayed there for the moment. She propped her guitar case against the wall and headed out onto the driveway. Tick pulled their bass out of the car and smiled at her. Their short blue streaked hair waved in the wind. Clare thought it suited them perfectly. She liked it better than the red.

"Have you checked your phone?" Tick asked as she put her bass in the garage.

"No." She looked at her phone. Keon and Spencer both texted they were running late. "Ah. Are you hungry?"

"Nah. You?"

"No. I had a snack in the car. Keon's schedule doesn't leave room for an early dinner."

"Who else is here?" They referenced the other cars. "Is it just Emma and Maggie?"

"There are two others with Emma. I didn't recognize them. She said they were going to check the enclosure for problem spots."

"Do you like it here? I mean, the house is nice, but the property is so big. You've always lived in the city, right?"

"I do miss the city, but I love being out here. I haven't been here long, but there's a spot in the back beside the stream that is my favorite."

Tick checked their watch. "Can I see it? We have time."

"You really want to? Yeah." Clare could feel the stupid grin on her face.

She practically jogged to the spot through the woods, way past the designated backyard section. Tick kept up with her, no problem. The two of them discussed the songs they wanted to add to the group's repertoire as they walked.

Clare pushed through the low-hanging branches and stepped out to the stream. The temperature dropped slightly this close to the river under the canopy. She crouched down and dipped her hands in the water. She wondered how much the water temperature dropped in the winter. Savannah didn't get cold, not like Pennsylvania.

Tick crouched beside her. "It is beautiful here. I bet you could get a few animals to approach you if you stay still enough."

"Maybe. I'll try it. If it works, I'll credit you with turning me into a princess." She laughed and splashed Tick.

"Hey." They splashed back. "I don't think that will work out. Spencer's not exactly a prince."

"Prince Spencer of the pack. Protector of the blood bank," Clare said in a deep voice, then stood up. "Oh god. Are vampires real?"

"Yeah, but they are not really around here. I'm not sure why or even if it's a sizeable population."

"What about faeries?"

Tick threw a rock into the stream, then stood. "Yep. You can see them from time to time. They are small and look like colorful flying insects, but only those of us with a connection to the supernatural can see them."

"I saw something like that at Maggie's." She grinned. "It's nice to find a place I belong."

Tick pulled her into a half hug. "You're not wrong."

Their fingers dug into her shoulder. "Tick, what's wrong?"

"Did you hear that?" They let go of her.

Clare stopped moving and listened. "No," she whispered.

"Something's wrong."

Tick took off through the woods faster than Clare could run. She wasn't sure what they heard, but she knew she would never catch up to the shifter, even in human form. As she jogged back, she felt Spencer get closer, then fear and anger flooded their bond.

She picked up the pace. Pain came next. How dare someone hurt her Spencer. Before she broke through the trees into the backyard, she picked up a stick she passed on the ground.

Maggie and Emma stood back-to-back, using what looked like short swords to fight two large men. Spencer's car sat in the background, both front doors open. She spotted the white nose of his brown wolf growling at what she could only call a lizard man. A dark brown wolf with silver feet and nose stood against an almost orange mountain lion and someone who shot sparks.

Both wolves were further away, so she stuck to the edge of the trees to center herself on the back of the man attacking Maggie. *I'm a bad bitch*, she thought before she snuck up behind the man and swung the branch at his legs using the knowledge she got from little league softball. He toppled, and she ran for the garage.

She almost tripped over a dazed Tick face-first on the ground. She half dragged them along.

Behind her, Maggie cried, "Clare! Scream!"

She bumped into the two people Emma had brought over for the fence inspection. "You two, close your ears."

Clare turned toward the fight and took a deep breath. "AAAHHHHHH!"

The yell lasted longer than she expected. The two men on Emma and Maggie fell to the ground, gripping their ears. She turned away before she could see what happened. The cry brought the others to the ground, including Spencer and the other wolf.

"We have to help them," the lady with short blonde hair said.

"Can't you shift?"

The man beside her with long brown hair said, "We weren't born werewolves."

"Can any of you fight like Emma?"

They all shook their heads.

Tick pulled up on her and the wall. "Sing."

Clare helped support them. "What?"

"Sing. 'Least of My Kind.' Sing it loud."

"Will it work?"

"I hope so. Get ready to shift, you two." Tick took off their clothes.

Clare's heart pounded. Would her words work? Spencer and the other wolf needed the help, and she wasn't sure what Maggie and Emma were doing. But what if it didn't work? Tick's glare snapped her out of her thoughts.

She opened her mouth and sang.

"Think on the battle-cost; this time the wolf has lost

Beaten and broken and blind.
Better beware, my lord; better prepare, my lord;
I was the least of my kind."

Tick's change happened the fastest. Her light gray wolf with black feet darted out to help the wolf with silver feet. The guy with the long hair's transition began, but wasn't finished.

"Prying my switchblade cold out of my fingers' hold,
Pause to take stock, reflect, and rue.
Look on the damage done here by a single one;
What do you think a full pack will do?"

As she entered the chorus again, his shift ended. His coloring matched a calico cat, but he was as fierce as the other wolves fighting. He took off to help the others. She turned to the blonde. She hadn't shifted and shrugged at Clare.

"Should I keep singing?" Clare asked.

"No. My wolf likes the song, but we've never heard it before."

A piercing pain in her chest brought her attention back to the battle. Spencer's wolf rolled away from the lizard man. Clare ran toward him. She faintly heard someone calling her name, but Spencer needed her.

She kneeled next to him. His eyes looked up at her, and he started to fight her. She could feel his worry, but she wouldn't leave him. The lizard man prowled their way. His pale mug faded into green and brown scales around the edges, and a long tongue flicked in and out of his mouth. One of his brown scaly hands twirled a tire iron. He smirked at her before he lunged at them. She covered her mate's ear and screamed.

The man clutched his ears and fell. Behind him, she saw Tick's wolf and the dark brown wolf sprint toward them. Clare pulled Spencer's body away as the two other wolves slammed into the man. His screams reverberated through the trees. She kept her face down toward the white heart on his nose. She didn't want to see what happened to the lizard man.

Spencer wiggled under her and licked her nose. "Gross," she told him.

He managed to get onto all four feet and walked in the house's direction. Clare followed beside him. She stroked his fur as he hobbled along, one of his legs obviously injured.

Emma and Maggie stared down at the tied-up man. He struggled against the restraints and tried to yell through his gag. Emma punched him on the side of the head. He whimpered, but stopped moving.

"Hayley, go inside and grab clothes for the wolves to change into," Emma said to the girl with the short, blonde hair.

She ran inside while the four wolves shifted back into their human skin. The dark brown wolf with silver feet changed into Keon. Clare averted her eyes from the naked people now standing before them.

Spencer turned her head to look at him. He smiled and caressed her cheek. "You saved me."

"I didn't save you. I distracted him long enough for someone else to come."

"You still came for me." He rubbed his nose on hers.

"Of course I did." She put a hand on his side and felt something sticky. Her hand came back covered in blood. It encased his other arm as well. "You're bleeding."

"It's my arm. No worries."

"Are you kidding me?" It suddenly felt hard to breathe. There was too much blood loss. She looked around at the rest of the group. Everyone sported cuts and bruises. "Is it always like this?"

Hayley ran outside with a bundle of clothes in one arm and a large tackle box in the other. Keon took the clothes while she kneeled and opened up the box to reveal first aid materials. She handed out packs of gauze, wound wash solution, and more. Everyone started cleaning themselves up. Hayley helped the others, but Clare focused on Spencer.

"You should help the others," he whispered.

"You're hurt the worst. What were you thinking?"

"Me? What about you? You went after that guy with a tree branch. You can't do that if you don't know what you're doing."

"You'll have to teach me then," she huffed, wrapping his arm the best she could. "You need stitches."

"Emma will do it later."

It didn't take long for everyone to bring their attention back to the man tied at Emma's feet.

"What happened to the others?" Clare asked.

Everyone looked around at each other, avoiding Clare's eyes. Spencer pulled her close and whispered into her ear, "They're dead."

"Oh." She didn't have anything else to say. What

could she say? Her shoulders relaxed receiving the news, yet her stomach twisted as well.

Emma pulled up on the man's collar, took off his gag, and looked into his eyes. "Who are you?"

He spat at her. "I will never tell you," he said in a high-pitched voice.

She wiped her face off with the sleeve of her shirt. Her eyes glowed, and she growled. Spencer's arm tightened around Clare's waist.

"In case you didn't notice, you're the only one left alive." Emma let go of his collar. The sound of his head hitting the ground made several of the party flinch. "Or you could answer my questions."

Keon walked back to the group. Clare wondered when he walked away. He stood beside Emma with his hands on his hips. "Looks like they are from Cernunnos. The others all have a tattoo on their chest."

Emma pulled down the man's shirt and showed everyone his tattoo of a circle with an opening on the bottom and a bow and arrow pointing up on the left side of his chest. She poked it a few times and let go of his shirt.

"Got tired of waiting on the bounty hunters to do your dirty work?"

"You don't know anything."

Maggie laughed. It quickly turned to hysterics as she sat on the ground in a fit of giggles.

"We know you're looking for a book we don't have. We know you want Maggie for whatever reason. And we know your leader wants to suck the world dry of its magic." Emma's attention stayed on the man. "Do you have anything else to say?"

"I already told you everything." She could barely hear his voice, though Clare thought the wolves heard it clear as day.

"Maggie, if you could get yourself together, can you put this man to sleep?" Emma closed her eyes. "Hayley, can you call Jesi and ask her to come here as soon as possible? Tell her not to bring Chuck."

Maggie crawled away, still full of laughter, and returned a few minutes later, more composed, with a small pouch in her hand. With a tear-stained face, she sprinkled the contents of the pouch over the man and whispered something Clare couldn't hear. His eyes rolled into the back of his head, and he started snoring loudly.

"Jesi's on her way," Hayley said.

Clare wondered why they needed Jesi and not Sylvia or Ethan. And how would they handle the dead bodies? Some weren't even human. Maybe none of them were human. She turned, buried her face into Spencer's chest, and sunk into his warmth. His arm looked bad. She didn't want to think about what could have been.

Chapter 26

Spencer

Spencer rubbed his cheek on the top of Clare's head. Leaves stuck out of her hair. He picked them out one at a time. Having her in his arms now helped calm him down.

His stomach dropped when he saw her exit the tree line with that branch. He instantly understood why bonded couples tried not to join the same fight. Any distraction could end in disaster, like the first slash to his arm.

That daeserpium or demon serpent had some nasty claws. Of course, he wasn't exactly a demon. Human hybrids existed and were often wrongly associated with evil and the devil. He'd never encountered a lizard hybrid before, though he'd read about them.

The pain brought him back to the fight. Watching Tick run by as a wolf both confused him and gave him hope. He ignored the human and continued to fight. He couldn't let anyone else get close to Maggie or Clare. The speed of the man he fought increased. After another slash to his hurt arm and a kick to the side, he rolled away, unable to catch his breath.

Panic consumed him when Clare showed up at his side. But she stopped the demon serpent long enough for help to arrive and for him to breathe normally.

He let her press her face against him as he rubbed her back. The pack didn't fight regularly, but he'd seen enough battles not to be shaken. He never wanted Clare to see one again.

He watched Emma make a call and then come back to the group. She began giving orders to everyone. Cops arriving were unlikely, but not out of the realm of reality.

"Clare," he whispered. "Why don't you go inside and clean up? Leave your dirty clothes in the bathroom." He didn't want to tell her they might have to burn them.

"I want to help," she mumbled into his skin.

"What?"

She lifted her face and turned toward Emma. "I want to help. What can I do?"

Emma gave her a half smile. "Help Maggie. She'll tell you what to do."

Clare gave him a quick kiss, then walked to Maggie. He knew his job well. While the other piled the bodies together for cleansing and burning, he went around and marked all the spots that had blood. His sense of smell worked better than most others in human form. After that, he'd search for their transportation.

With one attacker still alive, Jesi could glean his life's story. He always liked Ms. Oblena's power to know a person's story with a touch. After she died, the power moved to Jesi. He didn't understand the intricacies of magic, but Maggie told him everyone considered that gift dangerous and only one person had that power at a time. Knowledge really was power.

He knew Ethan would be there soon as well. Emma wouldn't call anyone else. He'd decide on what to do with the last man standing. Maybe they'd send him back with a message. Or maybe death. Whatever the case, he hoped the decision made stopped the attacks on Maggie.

It took two hours to mark all the blood spots and locate the hunter's vehicle. Honestly, the car wasn't hard to find. When he returned to the house, the sun sat low in the sky, and the floodlights around the place lit up the area. Ethan, Isaiah, and Sally walked out of the house and over to Emma and the sleeping captive. Spencer jogged up to the group to listen.

Ethan nodded at the group. "We've decided to send a message through this...person."

"Is that a good idea? Do you think he'll deliver it?" Emma asked.

"We were wondering if Maggie can guarantee he delivers it in person." Ethan looked around the yard. "Where is she?"

"She's upstairs with Jesi. They are getting rid of the latent tracking spell. I've never seen her look so ashamed. Seems they hired someone to put one on her before the bounty went up. None of us or the coven ever noticed." Emma looked toward the house as she spoke.

"Should we call Sylvia?" Isaiah sniffed the air and looked at their hostage. "He's a human?"

Emma nodded. "Let's ask Maggie who would be best." She pulled out her phone and sent a message.

After a few minutes of exchange, Emma turned to Spencer. "Can you ask Clare to come here?"

~

Clare

Clare followed Spencer to the group outside. She shifted her weight from foot to foot with all eyes on her.

"Clare, Maggie thinks that having a Siren charm this gentleman to send a message is our best option. Do you have a way of contacting them?"

"No, I don't..." Her eyebrows shot up. "I do. I forgot."

She pulled the bird necklace from under her shirt and rubbed the lapis stone. While she rubbed, she thought 'Will a Siren please help?' Her ammachi didn't tell her how long to rub, so she continued for five minutes.

Everyone looked around after she dropped the necklace. She shrugged. "I don't know how long it will take or if anyone will answer."

Spencer took hold of her hand. He kissed it, sending tingles down her arm. His eyes held a soft glow, so she knew his wolf was near the surface. She could wait all day as long as he stood beside her.

"Do you hear that?" Sally looked into the backyard.

"Yes. Someone's coming." Ethan watched the tree line.

Clare didn't hear anything and followed everyone's gaze. She couldn't see anything in the darkness and felt silly for trying.

"It's your ammachi," Spencer said.

"Really?" She took off in the direction of his stare. Sure enough, her ammachi walked into the backyard with a giant smile. The blue sari she wore barely touched the ground.

"Oh, my sweet child." She wrapped Clare in a hug.

"I thought you went home."

"I could not leave just yet. I knew you would need me soon."

Clare walked her back to the group and introduced her to those she hadn't met.

After learning the situation, her ammachi nodded. "I agree to your request. But I can't stay much longer. I told my husband I'd be back soon."

Clare pouted. "Are you sure?"

"Yes, you're in excellent hands." She turned to Ethan. "What message are you sending?"

Chapter 27

Roderic

A man walked into Roderic's office and averted his eyes from the man in charge of Cernunnos, who stood in front of him. A sneer crossed Roderic's lips and his pinched tipped nose flared at the sight of the slashes on his subordinate's body.

Roderic looked at the man in his blood-stained clothes. "Kneel."

He kneeled with a slight moan. While his wounds no longer bled, it still pained him to move.

"And your report, Gunther?" Roderic's arms rested on the small of his back, his eyes narrowed.

"I'm the only survivor."

"I wonder why you returned at all, then."

"I didn't have a choice," he squeaked out.

"Is that so?" He drew out his words and walked around the man. "Pray tell, why not?"

"A spell. I have a message. I had to come."

Roderic kicked him. He screamed and fell, holding his

side.

"You dare enter this building while knowingly under a spell?" he yelled.

Gunther curled into a ball, holding his ears. "I'm compelled. The message."

Roderic picked up the man and placed him in a chair. He dusted Gunter's shoulders and knees off. "I'm terribly sorry. What is this message?"

"Th...The message. Is...is 'You de...desire a book we do not have. Th...this is the ll...last time we leave a survivor.'"

"Who gave you this message?" He put a finger under Gunther's chin, forcing him to look up.

"A man. Older."

"A witch?"

"A wolf, I think."

"And the five of you were defeated by...?"

"Both. Mostly wolves. One witch's yell made our ears bleed."

Roderic frowned. "How many of each? Think about it before you answer."

The man shook before him. "Tw...Two witches. And four, no, five wolves."

"Seems I've underestimated the bond between their coven and the local pack." He let go of his face, walked to the phone on his desk, and picked up the receiver. "Yes. Send someone to sterilize Gunther. Now."

Gunther's cries echoed in the room. "Please, no. Don't. It hurts so bad."

"We must get that nasty magic off of you. And you

need to relearn your oath." He picked at his nails, no longer interested.

"But I didn't tell them anything."

"You didn't die for the cause either." He wrapped his large hand around Gunther's neck. "I should have sent Andre."

Chapter 28

Spencer

Over a week passed without an attack. Nothing nefarious happened during the full moon and the pack's concert delighted the group, though they had to keep the set short because of injuries. Even with fast healing, the three wolves in the band still felt sore. Spencer took the mic when it came time to play "Least of My Kind."

Sylvia's contact confirmed that the bounty never returned and shared a rumor that those who placed the bounty retreated in fear. Spencer didn't believe fear had anything to do with it. Retreating only meant regrouping.

But today, he put all thoughts of hunters out of his mind. Maggie moved home, and Clare agreed to move in with him. The coven finished all the protective shields on Maggie's home and shop. Next week, they agreed to create a warning system on his property.

Clare dropped her last box on the dining room table. "Now it's time to move it all upstairs."

"I wanted to talk to you about that." He rubbed the

back of his neck. "I know we agreed to live together, but I don't want to force you to live in the same room."

"Oh, I just assumed we would." She frowned.

He smiled. "Well, my room is a little small. I thought we could move into a larger room."

"...okay." She stood with her hands on her hips.

He grabbed her hand and pulled her upstairs. "Let me show you."

At the top of the stairs, he turned left, away from his door. At the end of the hall, he opened the last door and led her inside. The walls were painted a light teal color, except for one wall, which was a dark teal. The only furniture in the room was a bed next to the accent wall. Over the last few years, he slowly cleaned this room out when he had the time. In case someone needed it, he wanted it to be available.

He watched Clare walk around the room and open the doors to the closet and the connected bathroom. The ceiling fan spun slowly as he looked up. He wished the room came with a vaulted ceiling, but knowing when the home was built, he felt content with the attached bathroom.

"I like it." She sounded quiet as she looked out one of the windows out over the backyard. "This was your parents' room?"

He nodded. "Yeah."

"Are you comfortable living here?" She moved to him and picked up one of his hands. "I don't want it to be weird for you."

"It's fine. In fact, it's perfect for us." He kissed her

hand and watched her smile grow. "We can change the paint color if you want. And the bed. And anything else. It's better to move into a place together rather than trying to find a spot in an already occupied space."

"What a smart man I've found." She pulled him into a kiss.

Her kiss filled his body with warmth. He wanted nothing more than to be with her all day, every day. He lifted her, and she wrapped her legs around his waist. His tongue found hers as he pressed her against a wall. One hand grabbed her plump bottom, and the other sunk into her smooth hair. The desire to take her against the wall overwhelmed him. She probably wouldn't mind, considering how she moved against his hardening member.

He kissed down her neck and breathed in her sweet scent. Her hands, which caressed his head and back, suddenly stopped. He followed her lead and stilled his movements.

"What's wrong?"

"Is that the bed your parents used?"

He looked over his shoulder at the naked bed. He hadn't even put sheets on it yet. "Yeah. Why?"

"I think we need to move a different bed in here." Her feeling of uneasiness slipped through the bond.

He couldn't help it. He laughed. "Okay. Not a problem."

With a kiss on her beautiful lips, he pushed away from the wall, still holding her tight, and walked out of the room.

"Where are we going?"

He nibbled her neck with a chuckle. "To a different bed."

Special Thanks to Catherine Faber

The lyrics to "Least of My Kind" are used with permission from Cat Faber.
You can find more music by Cat Faber here:
catfaber.bandcamp.com

The original recording of "Least of My Kind" can be found at:
echoschildren.bandcamp.com/track/least-of-my-kind

Acknowledgements

Thanks everyone for being patient with me this year. I know everyone wanted this book sooner.

Shout out to my beta readers. Without them, there would be more homophones and awkward sentences than a normal reader could take.

Special thanks to Christine, my sensitivity reader and inspiration for Clare. I'm so glad we were roommates for so long.

Extra special thanks to Cat Faber for allowing me to use "Least of My Kind" in this book. I love the lyrics so much and am honored I get to use them as part of this story. Everyone should listen to her music.

Thanks to my ARC group. I have found a wonderful group of people. You're support and enthusiasm encourages me every day.

Did you enjoy this book?

Please review and visit Lucille's website for updates, sign up for her newsletter, and learn how to find her across social media.

www.lucilleyateswrites.com

Also by Lucille Yates

A Bite of Magic Saga

The Wolf's Bite
The Witch's Complement
The Wolf's Return
The Wolf's Song

Corporate Shifters

For the Good of the Clan

About the Author

Lucille Yates writes paranormal romance and urban fantasy stories. They feature strong-willed women, complicated men, and sizzling chemistry.

Lucille enjoys writing the stories that are constantly playing like a movie in her head. She is excited that others will now enjoy them as much as she does.

When she is not writing, she is reading, playing with her son, watching videos, or playing games. She lives outside of Savannah, GA with her husband, son, and three cats.

The Carrier's Dilemma - A Bite of Magic Book 4 Coming Spring 2023.